DISCRETION

FAÏZA GUÈNE is an award-winning French Algerian writer and director. Spotted at a writing workshop at the age of thirteen, she went on to make an astonishing literary debut with *Kiffe kiffe demain* (Just Like Tomorrow), which was an international bestseller and has been translated into more than twenty-five languages. Her other novels in English (also translated by Sarah Ardizzone to critical acclaim) include *Dreams from the Endz*, *Bar Balto* and *Men Don't Cry*. Guène has directed several short films and is a co-writer on Disney+ Star's *Oussekine* (BAFTA-nominated for best international TV drama). In 2022 Faïza was made an International Fellow of the Royal Society of Literature.

Sarah Ardizzone is an award-winning translator from the French. She has received the Scott Moncrieff Prize twice for her translations of Faïza Guène's novels, with *Men Don't Cry* and *Just Like Tomorrow*, which was also shortlisted for the Young Minds Book Award. Ardizzone's other authors include Gaël Faye, Yasmina Reza, Daniel Pennac and Alexandre Dumas. She was made a Chevalier de l'Ordre des Arts et des Lettres in 2022.

'Guène's Paris is a place of grifting and grafting where young rebels rub up against calcified traditions. This is a writer at the height of her powers, addressing issues of migration and belonging with defiance, zest and humour.' **Bidisha**

'Guène has a fine eye for the contradictions, agonies and delights of life at the intersection of Algeria, contemporary Paris, and its banlieue. *Discretion* ... takes in dispossession,

belonging, memory and the intergenerational conflict over silence and discretion in the face of pain or injustice. A short bitter-sweet read with a light touch, Guène captures many of the tensions that tug at second-generation immigrant families in France today with honesty, humour and warmth.'
The Economist

'The thread on which this understated but haunting novel hangs is the idea that, even if one generation smothers its rage, it will re-emerge in the next ... Clear-eyed but tender, every page is filled with insight. A searching portrait of the desire for identity and acceptance, its recognition of bone-deep discrimination and injustice is biting.' *The Herald*

'Guene writes with poetic prose that reveals detailed glimpses into the generations of the Taleb family, hardened and shaped by war, immigration and racism.' *The National*

Faïza Guène

Discretion

Translated from French by Sarah Ardizzone

SAQI

Saqi Books
26 Westbourne Grove
London W2 5RH
www.saqibooks.com

First published in hardback 2022 by Saqi Books

This paperback edition published 2023

First published in French as *La discrétion* by Éditions Plon in 2020

Copyright © Éditions Plon, un département de Place des Éditeurs 2020
Translation © Sarah Ardizzone 2022

Faïza Guène has asserted her right under the Copyright, Designs
and Patents Act, 1988, to be identified as the author of this work.

Frantz Fanon extract on p. 115 © Translated by Constance Farrington

A full CIP record for this book is available from the British Library.

ISBN 978 0 86356 976 0
eISBN 978 0 86356 447 5

Printed and bound in Great Britain by Clays Ltd, Elcograf S.p.A.

This book is supported by the Institut français (Royaume-
Uni) as part of the Burgess programme, and by the Institut
français's 'Programme d'aide à la publication'.

This book has been selected to receive financial assistance from English PEN's
'PEN Translates!' programme, supported by Arts Council England. English
PEN exists to promote literature and our understanding of it, to uphold
writers' freedoms around the world, to campaign against the persecution and
imprisonment of writers for stating their views, and to promote the friendly
co-operation of writers and the free exchange of ideas. www.englishpen.org

To my mother
To all our mothers

It demands great spiritual resilience not to hate the hater whose foot is on your neck, and an even greater miracle of perception and charity not to teach your child to hate.

James Baldwin, *The Fire Next Time*

Yamina is coming up for seventy. She will reach this age in November of next year. On either the tenth or the nineteenth of the month. Yamina was born *one day or the other*.

According to her Algerian documents, it was the nineteenth, but her French residence permit, issued in Seine-Saint-Denis, states: 'Born 10 November 1949 at Msirda Fouaga, Algeria'.

Who to trust?

At least she has been spared a *presumed* birthdate, the notorious 1 January, assigned, by default, to colonised subjects.

Passengers are quick to offer Yamina their seat on the 173 bus, which she catches every Saturday morning from Fort d'Aubervilliers métro station, opposite the post office.

She is off to the Mairie d'Aubervilliers market to make all sorts of pointless purchases. Plastic tat and 'revolutionary' kitchen gadgets mainly, peddled by hawkers in headsets up on their platforms. Yamina could watch these shows for hours, enthralled. She sometimes claps in wonder at the end of a demo, even if the result is far from convincing – her trusting nature means she has no sense of being hoodwinked. Such an idea would never occur to her.

She wants to believe in the miracle demonstrated with fervour by the trader with the gift of the gab. It comes easily: no arm twisting is needed. She's ready to take this cheery Von Dutch-cap-wearing traveller at his word, despite the speed of his patter as he extols the magic of the all-purpose peeler.

The self-appointed preacher of Aubervilliers market always uses the same opening gambit on the shoppers gathered before his stand: 'M'sieurs, dames, bonjour! My name is Moses, and I'm God's right-hand comrade-in-arms!' Broad-chested and short-legged, the street vendor stands rooted to the spot. His fingers never brush the hands of the women he showers with small change, his hairy forearm flaunting a home-made tattoo: *Pour toi, Suzie.*

Yamina sets off again, convinced she's scooped a gadget *and* bagged the deal of the century.

The Mairie d'Aubervilliers market is an important ritual for Yamina. She heads there on her own, enjoying chance encounters with some of her girlfriends, avoiding others. Especially *the journalists,* which is her nickname for those who ask too many questions: 'What about your daughters? Still no marriage prospects?' Polite to a fault, Yamina defers to destiny: 'God will decide.'

Yamina hurries to catch the 173 in the opposite direction, the family ritual of Saturday lunch on her mind. The flourish with which she flashes her freedom pass – the driver giving her Navigo Forfait Amethyste card a cursory glance through tinted lenses – owes a debt to the detectives in her favourite TV series.

When people offer to give up their seat for her, she refuses at first: 'Non merci, it's kind of you, but I'm fine,' indicating she's capable of standing upright in the middle of the bus, wedged between two pushchairs. As if her balance won't be in jeopardy, as if the bend in rue Danielle Casanova won't swing her about. Not that she takes umbrage at being offered a seat on the basis of her age, not at all, she appreciates politeness. She just doesn't want to cause any bother. You have to make a point of insisting before she'll say yes. It's the same with the youths smoking cheap hash at the foot of her building, when they offer to carry her shopping upstairs: 'I'll be fine, my children, I can cope.'

They understand not to take no for an answer, they're used to her, and still they have to wrestle the bags out of her hands. She gives in with a smile but thanks them all the way to the threshold. She is touched by their help, remarking before she closes the door: 'You're good boys!'

The prospect of growing old does not frighten Yamina. She made her peace with it years ago, and appears unaffected by the tribulations of old age.

Yamina never complains.

It is as if that option was excised at birth.

And yet she is not without health problems, and must remember to take her pills twice a day to control her diabetes and blood pressure. Every couple of months, she visits the Lamarque laboratory on rue Helène Cochennec to run her blood tests. She takes the results to the doctor who's been her GP since 2003. The surgery is located in an old-fashioned house, at the end of a cul-de-sac. There are no appointments, you drop in and wait, sometimes for hours. Magazines with titles such as *Challenges* or *Management* are strewn on the dusty coffee table, along with an old copy of *L'Express*. On the cover, a scrawled-over portrait of former prime minister Manuel Valls, his eyes aggressively scratched out and a moustache added in biro.

Management and *Challenges*? Who wants to read business magazines in this neighbourhood? Nobody here identifies as the target audience. More's the pity, given one headline: 'Making it in France: you can do it and here's how!'

Best case scenario: someone stands up, scans the coffee table and sits back down again, disappointed.

In the consulting room, the doctor does the minimum, offering little beyond a routine examination.

What's striking is that when he speaks to Yamina he addresses her informally as *tu*, not because they're in any way close, or because he's an especially friendly doctor. No, he adopts this casual tone after calling her Madame Yamina.

For example: 'Now, now, Madame Yamina, have we been taking our little pills?' Or: 'The diabetes isn't looking tip-top today, Madame Yamina. Have we been putting too much sugar in our mint tea?'

Absurd as it may seem, Yamina is fond of him. Force of habit, probably. She's been coming here for fifteen years. She keeps the faith. The idea of deserting her GP has never crossed her mind. Her eagerness to ask after the doctor's own health borders on the comical.

She is, in all likelihood, the only one of his patients to enquire how he is doing, or to press for news of his family, and she does so with unsettling sincerity.

She detects nothing patronising in his tone. Not even when, under the guise of humour, he requests that she bare her ears, which are covered by her headscarf, so he can inspect them with his otoscope: 'Come on, let's take off our little burka, shall we, to show our little ears?'

Yamina sees no harm in this. It almost makes her smile.

Nor does Yamina see what these clumsy gestures betray. She doesn't register that the doctor is brusque and cursory. Sometimes, he knocks her when he lifts her arm to take her blood pressure, but she would never dare point this out. As if being hurt were acceptable. As if nothing really matters, where she is concerned.

Viewed from one angle, Yamina has been preserved. She hasn't grasped the geometry in which the world has placed her. Her innocence protects her from the violence behind the doctor's attitude. She doesn't notice the vertical relationship playing out in the surgery of someone she holds in high esteem, on account of his title, his years of study and his knowledge. She doesn't see the invisible ladder on which he perches every time he speaks to her.

Which begs the question of whether this is deliberate on Yamina's part, for she seems unfeasibly deaf to the call of anger. Perhaps she has chosen not to be destroyed by the scorn of others? Perhaps Yamina realised, long ago, that if she reacted to each and every provocation there would be no end to the matter?

Yamina's father was a resistance fighter. Over there, in Algeria. What if, today, for this woman approaching seventy, refusing to give in to resentment were, in itself, a form of resistance?

Except that anger, even when buried, doesn't disappear. Anger is passed on, without anyone realising it.

Her children have no time for such treatment. They can't bear their mother being spoken to as if she were totally gaga and naturally inferior.

They know who she is, and what she's lived through, and they demand that the whole world know this too.

Take the scene Hannah made the other day at the prefecture.

The official began by talking loudly and slowly from behind the glass partition, over-articulating her words for Yamina's benefit, as if scolding a child. Something about a missing document. Prompting Hannah, the most sensitive of Yamina's offspring, to retort: 'She's not an idiot. You don't need to talk to her like that.'

And so, protected by her screen, by the notice reminding the public that action will be taken against any threatening or abusive behaviour, protected by her status as a local government worker, protected by the fact that nobody wants to come back the following day to rejoin this wretched queue, the official doesn't deign to look Hannah in the eye.

'Hel-lo,' she sighs in exasperation, 'let's keep a lid on it, shall we? You people are always the same!'

This is all it takes to light the spark in Hannah. To make her feel the sulphur fizzing through her body. Weirdly, she can recall the relevant chemistry lesson: *An element with the symbol S. It belongs to the chalcogens and is insoluble.*

Hannah wants to cry. Each time someone patronises her mother, it is as if Yamina shrinks before her eyes, like a garment washed at high temperature.

Hannah senses the bile rising, at imminent risk of spilling over. There is so much anger inside her throat that it leaves a bitter taste of ancient anger, increasingly hard to contain. But crying means showing weakness, and that's out of the question. She is done with weakness.

'Who d'you think you're talking to?'

Hannah bangs on the screen while Yamina tries in desperation to restrain her.

'Binti, my daughter, it doesn't matter. Calm down.'

The woman behind the counter huffs and puffs again,

producing a gob of saliva which sticks to the screen. She, for one, can't see what the problem is. *It's always the same with these people. They're never happy!* Hasn't she, a public servant, gone above and beyond her job description – to be understood, to be generous? *What have I done wrong this time? Good grief, there's no knowing what they want!*

It's almost lunchtime and the official is hungry. Fabienne's stomach is making embarrassing gurgling noises. She's been out of sorts ever since she started on this high-protein diet, despite her high hopes a few weeks earlier when she bought Dr Jean-Michel Cohen's book, *Lose Weight Healthily*, from the Leclerc hypermarket by Normandie Niemen tramway.

She's trying to patch things up with Bruno, drop some weight, make herself more attractive for him, the way she was before. But Fabienne hardly thrives on deprivation, it makes her feel permanently tense.

For a while now, on top of counting the calories, she has been battling doubt. *What if there's another woman?* You think it only happens to other people. 'Stop getting ideas into your head, Fabienne,' he says, never looking up from his mobile phone. At first, she tried banishing these negative thoughts. But they've rapidly became a fixture: *Why's he started squirting the aftershave bottle fifty-three times when he always used to say perfume was for poofters?*

The thing about men is they lose interest, as she has frequently heard her mother remark, so she *has* been warned. They'll soon have been married for twenty-seven years. Long gone are the days of feeling a special glow every time his gaze rested on her. Back then, she believed in everlasting love and all that guff about true emotions.

Turns out Bruno is no different, just your average male. The spit of Mr Average.

Every couple they know is breaking into a thousand pieces. Half her girlfriends are divorced. So why should Fabienne be spared? She feels as if she's competing in On the Posts – one of those endgame challenges in *Survivor* – clinging on for dear life to avoid falling into the water. The prospect of being single again at fifty haunts her. To make matters worse, if it comes to it, she doesn't have a single flattering photo to post on a dating website.

Now, more than ever, Fabienne feels overlooked and fragile.

She had been so proud of becoming a local government worker. What a joke! She's paid for her years at the 'Pref' twice, maybe three times over. Just the sight of these dreary walls, the revolting building where she drags herself every morning, makes her feel sick. *Scratch Prefecture, this is a tomb. What suicide-triggering architect drew up these monstrous plans?* Fabienne has lost count of how many Combo Meal Deals she's gobbled at the McDonalds in Bobigny 2 shopping centre. Or her reluctant returns after lunchbreaks spent stirring a disgusting café crème at Segafredo, the café on the first floor of the shopping centre where scrawny ill-shaven men, nearly all of them North African, huddle.

The TV presenter Nagui, with his Egyptian–Italian

good looks, is the only Arab to win her approval. *He's not without charm* is her take on him, *twinkly eyes, not bad*. But those guys at Segafredo, they are the sort to make their wives do things. Fabienne pictures those women being made to do it, even on nights when they don't want to. *Of course, they're knackered most of the time anyway, because of their kids.*

Fabienne would put money on the men in the mall being wife-forcers, yes, that's it, *an army of forcers*. It makes her feel ill at ease. She doesn't dare glance at them, still less put her white arms on the café counter. *We'll soon have to pay for our coffee in dinars around here.*

She heads back to her desk with a dose of the blues, the kind that clings to the skin. *It's not for nothing Bobigny town centre is a terminus. Everything stops here. You want to be done with it all.*

Fabienne has had it up to here with this parade of races and dialects, of smashed-up faces and domestic stories that she'd rather not hear about. She is ill-equipped to deal with the paradoxes of these people: the gazes that smoulder while their hands beg, submissive shoulders belying clenched fists. Too much to understand, too many knots to unravel, plus that's not her job. They're behind a blurry screen, so why can't clients be blurry too? Fabienne is meant to ensure that procedures are followed. Not to take it on the jaw without flinching. *Fuck's sake!*

She jabs her finger at Hannah: 'Hey, you! Calm down, okay!'

The plump pink finger has inadvertently pressed an imaginary button, the red nuclear option.

'Nah, I won't calm down! Don't tell me to calm down! You'll speak to her with respect, you get me?'

Hannah is nitroglycerine, to be handled with care. Yamina understands this. She knows her daughter inside out. But Fabienne, with no prior knowledge, only makes matters worse.

'I'd like to remind you that you are speaking to a representative of the State!'

This is all it takes to ignite Hannah. She is ablaze now. Flaring up to defend her mother's honour.

'You think I give a damn you're an agent of the State? You think you're impressing anyone here? Like, who gives a shit!'

Once again, she bangs on the screen with the full length of her forearm.

'Fuck you, you fat bitch!'

The blind on the screen snaps shut. Fabienne goes off to lunch, wondering whether to call in sick, leaving Hannah in flames.

Security guards escort the pair off the premises. The mother hand-on-cheek from the shame of it, the daughter on the verge of exploding in the middle of Bobigny prefecture.

One of the guards, with his hi-vis orange armband, makes a show of sympathy. He addresses Yamina as Tata, Auntie, while steering her towards the exit. He's from the home country: you can tell by his accent. The respect he shows is comforting. But useless. He has no power.

His respect won't stop the day after from happening. Hannah will have to pay to park a second time before she and her mother cross the concourse and queue for hours. It might be just their luck to end up at Window C, meaning Fabienne's.

It isn't until she is sitting in her old blue Renault Clio, diesel, 2006, which she trawled for among the free classifieds and second-hand bargains on Leboncoin.fr, that Hannah notices her knees trembling. She reminds her mother to fasten her seatbelt since Yamina has a habit of ignoring her own safety.

Hannah catches her breath again. Her nerves are strained.

At least she didn't cry.

All Yamina can give her children is love.

Perhaps her love will soothe them.

With a little luck, it will make them forget the humiliations and unburden them of the sacrifices.

It is still mild for October. The window is wide open and

the curtain dances in the breeze. Yamina is grateful to be reuniting her family around the table for Saturday lunch.

In the kitchen, the pressure cooker is hissing deliciously: there's nothing in the world to beat it. The aroma wafts through the apartment. Yamina has prepared lamb with green beans: a dish her children adore, especially Omar. If happiness had a scent, it would be lamb on the simmer.

Her husband has dozed off on the living room banquette, in front of the television. It's a rerun of an old western from 1966: *El Dorado* with John Wayne and Robert Mitchum. Westerns are his favourites. Carefully, Yamina extricates the remote and tucks the cushion behind his neck.

Brahim Taleb is as handsome as ever, his skin remains radiant, his wrinkles like mysteries to be solved. He's no snorer. Yamina maintains he sleeps like the devout dead, which, coming from her, is high praise.

Standing in the middle of her traditional living room, she notes with pride that there's not a speck of dust showing on the ornaments, not a crease in the tablecloth. Now it's just a matter of waiting for her children so she can serve up. The table is already laid.

Yamina leans out of the fourth-floor window, her slim figure and stiff body discernible through her blue gandoura. She watches with affection the kids playing dodgeball outside. It seems only yesterday that her own children were playing beneath this window, without a care in the world, and she would call out their names to summon them back up to the apartment before darkness fell. Yamina sighs. She misses her kids.

It might not strike you at first, but behind Yamina there is a story and there is history, as for each and every one of us.

DOUAR OF ATOCHENE
PROVINCE OF MSIRDA FOUAGA
ALGERIA, 1949

This story begins somewhere in the west of Algeria.

At first glance, you might mistake it for an abandoned nomadic village or douar. Clucking red hens wander past the mournful gaze of a mule tethered to a fig tree.

There are barley fields all around, but the sky has shown no clemency this year, despite the inhabitants' fervent prayers for rain.

The traditional small stone house, known as a mechta, is bounded by Barbary figs, while the ridges and slopes across the region are dotted with cactus plants.

A heaviness in the air ties stomachs in knots. The last famine wasn't so long ago, and people still remember it. Everything seems precarious again. Perhaps there's a sense of foreboding about the ravages of a war to come, like the menace of an overcast sky.

Except there's no rain. There is still no rain.

Rising up, in the middle of the douar, is a house made

of tlakht: this is the clay taken from the mountainside, then mixed with barley bran to build walls. Inside, scant furniture, esparto grass matting on the beaten earth floor and bustling women.

Beads of sweat form beneath their coloured scarves. One of them chants, her voice clear and calm, and, if it weren't for the brown marks on her hands, it would be impossible to guess at her age. She remains unflustered. You need at least one. This village qabla, the official midwife, offers a reassuring presence, stroking the hand of Rahma, the pink-faced girl, to whom nothing has been explained.

As the pain distorts Rahma's vision, making her hallucinate, the Berber tattoos on the forehead of the crouching midwife begin to blur. Rahma frowns and stares at the limewashed walls, where she thinks she can see hundreds of lizards climbing in two columns. They look like the French soldiers she spotted catching frogs on the opposite bank of the oued, the river. Apparently, they eat frogs.

She had felt terrified, that day, picking up her pace, her breath quickening with her step. The soldiers exchanged banter, sniggering as they pointed at her taut, swollen belly. One of them whistled and signalled for her to approach. Rahma called on Allah for help as best she could, not being familiar with the correct turns of phrase. Unlike her brothers, she hadn't been given the opportunity of attending Quranic school.

Rahma's face hardened as she walked towards the

soldiers. She had learned not to show her fear, to be guarded about it. *They had taken their land, but they would not take their dignity.* She was losing her air of candour, and in its place was a solemn mask, one she would wear forever.

After a brief silence, the soldier jostled Rahma, jabbering in a language she didn't understand, and the bundle of clothes she was carrying on her head tipped over, tumbling at his feet. A glimmer of compassion crept into his eye: he was on the verge of picking up the clothes, then thought better of it. *To hell with her. Let her sort out her own bloody mess.* It wasn't like he'd done it on purpose. Just shoved her about a bit, *nothing to write home about.*

Algeria, these natives, the other officers' horror stories… what were they to him? Nineteen months already. He couldn't wait to return to Brignoles, never wanted to hear talk of Algeria again. Ever since the call-up, his life had been a nightmare. Antoine's only wish was to take over his father's garage and repair bodywork. He loved salvaging old jalopies and giving them a second flush of youth. Now that the towelheads, the bicots, had started rebelling, boys like him were being sent to Algeria, when, like everyone else, he'd never asked for it. Antoine was a softie, not given to intimidating women. He wanted to make his friends laugh, end of. *This is one shit-dull country – this bled – right? What a godforsaken land.*

And laugh they did when they saw the knocked-up bougnoule struggling to bend over and retrieve her laundry

– why take pity on a wog? Later, when he turned in for the night, Antoine thought back to the incident, recalling the look in the woman's shadowy eyes, and felt ashamed of his actions. Naturally, he kept his remorse to himself.

Nothing is more personal than regret.

Rahma had spent much of the day washing and drying the clothes in the sun, on the banks of the oued. Now, because of the frog-eaters, her laundry was dirty again, so she would have to return the following morning to start over.

This girl with plump pink cheeks is still of an age for playing. Something from Rahma's childhood clings to her as she plunges her bare white feet into the river, hopping and laughing, having first checked the other women aren't looking her way. She doesn't want them noticing how much she enjoys walking over the pebbles and watching the clear water pass between her toes. Rahma senses the cool freshness rising to the crown of her head, and it feels delicious.

And yet her childhood is over.

They made a woman of her *abruptly*.

Perhaps it's the same for women the world over.

Becoming a woman is sudden, from one moment to the next.

And the women of Msirda are not spared.

Rahma's future mother-in-law had noticed the girl scrubbing clothes on the banks of the river Kis, which separates Algeria from Morocco, and said: 'I'll take those pretty calves for my son.' Well-developed calves, thick and curvaceous, were considered a mark of beauty in those days. Lying on the matting, facing the qabla who is chanting now, Rahma tries to come to her senses. There are so few happy memories to draw on that might help take her mind off the pain.

She knows there are neither lizards nor soldiers on the wall. She tells herself it's probably the fever. She can feel someone sponging down her forehead.

A flash of pain pierces her belly and Rahma confuses her suffering with death, convinced the soul is being ripped out of her. She believes she is departing this life.

Imagine a cry.

A cry that splits the darkness of the night.

A cry that glances off the moon, before crashing into the sky, then bursts and falls back down again, like thousands of tiny lead balls. A cry that fills the douar, rudely awakening the villagers whose floating spirits return precipitously to their bodies.

The child is born.

A girl.

A girl with an uncertain destiny, like that of a country on the cusp of reclaiming its freedom.

Yamina was born in a cry.

So why choose to lead a silent existence?

RENAULT TALISMAN BUSINESS, DCI 1.5
ECO2 ENERGY (LEATHER INTERIOR)
PARIS (75006)
FRANCE, 2018

Crossing the rue du Bac, the weariness sets in. His arms are growing numb.

Omar doesn't much care for this part of the city, but he's still in the area tonight.

His drop-off was a little further up, at Hôtel Lutetia, where the renovations are finished at last. To his eyes the new facade looks sumptuous.

Staring at the building as it flaunted its new skin, he reflected that he might like to step inside one day. He could sit at the hotel bar and order something, a Coke perhaps. It wouldn't cost more than 10 euros, after all, no more than a pack of cigarettes, except it isn't about the money. No matter how much he earns, it still won't change anything. There's an indefinable barrier inside his head, and it's telling him he can't set foot inside the Lutetia.

Omar has always felt this way, as if it were in his blood, or in his stomach: *some things are not for the likes of us.* These things were made for others, for those who already have everything. For the people who've always had these things, without ever needing to ask for them. Without even having desired them. From the beginning these things were there for them. They are simply following an old and well-established rhythm.

Omar should engrave this on stone: *Others don't need to exclude us. We do a great job of it ourselves.*

The idea of stepping inside the fancy hotel briefly crossed his mind. Then Omar sighed and thought about something else.

He's wearing a midnight-blue suit from Zara, perfectly ironed. He was upbeat the day he bought it, noting his handsome appearance in the changing room mirror. It gave him presence. But, as for so many other Uber drivers, the pay proved poor and his enthusiasm rapidly fizzled out.

Dawn is breaking, the birds are already making a racket. He decides that this job here, at Sèvres-Babylone, will be his last pick-up of the night.

There's no bottled water inside the Renault Talisman, no mints, no dangling air freshener. It's been a while since Omar gave up on replenishing his stocks. He earns too little to fork out from his own pocket.

In the backseat, two American tourists gush *amazing* and

awesome on repeat at the spectacle Paris offers them. They wear outsize hoodies stamped with their university, teamed with tiny denim shorts. *Could someone explain why American girls feel the cold everywhere except for on their legs?*

One of them plays with her ponytail. She's not pretty, no, there's something ungainly about her features. Her complexion is a greasy pink, her over-wide nostrils reveal ruddy-coloured nasal passages and her profile is pudgy. Her high-pitched voice doesn't help.

But as Omar catches a view of this American girl, it occurs to him that his mother would find her pretty. He can picture her inspecting the girl's pale face, examining her blue eyes and blonde hair, and expressing her approval at this doll: 'Poupiya!'

For Yamina, being beautiful means being white, blonde and blue-eyed. This is a given, as far as she's concerned, no questions asked. And yet, having carefully scrutinised this girl's face, Omar can confirm that no, she's not beautiful, although he'd put money on her being a hit at the village hammam.

'Eez okay the music for you girlz? You la-ike Djazz?' asks Omar in an English that's clumsy and broken, to the point, almost, of being dirty. American ponytail couldn't care less. 'Whatever,' she shrugs, scarcely glancing in Omar's direction. She sprawls on the seat, turning to the other blonde: 'I am soooo hungry!' She'd kill for a hamburger dripping with cheese and ketchup.

She and her friends have been out drinking white wine

– Chablis, 'Oh gosh! French wine is soooo good!' – but not to the point of excess. Just as well. Omar loathes the weekend shifts for this reason. He can't be dealing with zombies, catching their disturbing glassy eyes in the rear-view mirror, listening to their senseless blathering, or performing emergency stops in the bus lane so they can throw up. Drunk people disgust him. 'Fuck's sake, get a grip,' he wants to say, but bites his lip.

It's only short-term, in any case. The steering wheel, the passengers, the stench of nocturnal piss, the Zara suit, the job, *it's all temporary*. He repeats this like a mantra. In the beginning, it helped make everything seem more bearable, but, truth be told, he's no longer convinced.

When does a gig cease to be temporary? How do you gauge the switch from *temporary* to *permanent*? You slide without realising it. Because, the thing is, this short-term job's already gone on for two years. He'll soon be thirty, and he's worried.

He likens it to when he started to lose his hair. He used to think that was short-term, too. Omar had been well-endowed in this respect, killer curls, not so much black as chestnut. He remembers the rigmarole with the shampoo, how he got it to lather, the sensation of damp hair drying naturally. He put his sudden hair loss down to stress, and splashed out on exorbitant scalp treatments from the discount pharmacy at Parinor shopping centre. When the first bouts of hair loss exposed his pate, his big sister Hannah teased him, calling him Pebble Head. He used a pocket mirror to inspect the back, checking on progress, taking clumsy photos on his iPhone 6 with its cracked screen. He even researched cosmetic tourism, looked into trips to Turkey offering capillary implants at unbeatable prices. There were some eye-boggling before and after pics on the websites. But then he felt ashamed and scrubbed his search history from the home computer.

One day, Omar simply stopped looking. He came to terms with his balding destiny. He would be bald, just as his father had been bald before him, and his grandfather before them.

Baldness is another form of inheritance, after all, and it hadn't detracted from his charm. One lost hair at a time, Omar was turning into a short, balding Arab. A pebble head in a dark suit driving a Renault Talisman, a sympathetic face looking out from his photo in the 'driver profile' section of the app, just below the number of completed trips. Omar has already notched up thousands of journeys. Thousands of faces. Thousands of kilometres distancing him from his former ambitions. He won't let his life be reduced to this tally, to this suit made in some factory in South Asia, by workers even less well paid than he is, to this car, which he has to keep immaculate at all times to avoid negative feedback.

Omar was a good student at school, passing his exams, listening when they said he would have to fight twice as hard as the others. Which is precisely what he did. And then what?

It wasn't as though he was doing it to please his mother and father. Or to avenge the sacrifices they had made as exiles, or to rescue anybody from abject poverty. Omar's family has always had enough food on the table.

Yamina is proud of this son who drives a smart car and wears a suit. She reckons he's doing a lot better than some of her friends' sons, the ones who've done time inside, making their mothers submit to being frisked by prison guards before they can enter the visiting room. She reckons he's doing a lot better than the alkies and drugheads who beg outside the overground station with their flea-infested dogs.

Mainly she reckons he's doing a lot better than his father.

Before he retired, the head of the family was a formworker, or concrete carpenter. He was permanently exhausted and on edge, always telling tedious tales from the construction sites, the same tired stories involving pneumatic drills, Portuguese co-workers, back pain and unsympathetic bosses.

Back then, Brahim, Omar's father, was haunted by a recurring nightmare.

On a construction site, bustling workers. The smoke rising from ground level makes monstrous shapes, and the drains give off a foul smell. A giant tipper arrives to pour reinforced concrete. Brahim is tasked with this operation. At first he's proud of the responsibility and everything goes to plan, but, just as the pouring procedure begins, he realises that his children are trapped in the formwork. They're struggling to get out and there's nothing he can do. He puts his hands to his hard helmet and roars as he watches his kids drowning in the grey substance. Brahim feels powerless and to blame: his children are dying, before his eyes, it's his fault, he knows this, he's the one who brought them here in the first place. His children are losing their lives to concrete. It's a tragedy. One he didn't see coming. The concrete is an all-devouring beast and Brahim wants to die, he wants to be swallowed up in turn. He tries to join his children in the formwork, to sink with them, but he can't. His legs won't respond.

It ends like this.

With his kids, the children he loves so dearly, disappearing before his eyes into the concrete he himself has poured.

Omar's father used to wake with a jolt, drenched in sweat, grabbing his wife by the shoulder, even though she hated being woken like that in the middle of the night. Heart pounding, he would blurt out his nightmare in jumbled, incoherent snatches. His wife would look on in disbelief. 'This is crazy! All you think about is work. Recite the Throne verse and go back to sleep. It's four in the morning, it'll soon be time to get up.'

Brahim's work was backbreaking. At midday, he ate potatoes from a metal lunch pail. Every day of the week, without fail, potatoes in his lunch pail.

'Watch out, my son, work hard at school, or it'll be your turn to carry a lunch pail!' was how Omar's father encouraged him to knuckle down.

In Omar's childish mind, the lunch pail was a threat: of failure, of a life of hard labour.

The lunch pail meant ending up like his father.

Yamina had cooked enough potatoes in her time, filled enough lunch pails and cleaned enough mud-splattered boiler suits. Her hands were rough from scrubbing the dirty laundry under a cold tap. The grime from a construction site, the stains it leaves, are tough to eradicate. But today, when she looks at her family, she doesn't begrudge her efforts.

Yamina can feel her heart overflowing with emotion for them, *overflowing like the Mediterranean*. She has enough love for a hundred sons and daughters to share. The breast of this woman is devoid of any bitterness, which is in the order of a miracle when you think about it. Her children envy her this innocence, but they also chide her, on occasion, for being too forgiving.

Omar's mind often wanders while he's driving. He thinks about the past. And God knows, reflecting on the past is no easier than imagining the future. Omar thinks about all the love he's received, and that his sisters have received. He thinks about his parents, his mother's sad eyes, everything those eyes have seen, his father's big hands, everything those hands have lacked the opportunity to communicate. Omar thinks about everyone else, the people in transit, the exiled hearts, the dreams abandoned along the way. Will it be the same for his own dreams?

It's gone five now. The hour at which his father used to wake for the construction site. Omar decides it's time to head home. He switches off TSF Jazz after dropping the American girls at place de la Bastille. Then he closes the app and loosens his tie.

With a little luck, he'll make it back in time for the Fajr prayer at the mosque in Aulnay-Sous-Bois.

DOUAR OF ATOCHENE
PROVINCE OF MSIRDA FOUAGA
ALGERIA, 1954

Yamina is a skinny child. Her large honey-coloured eyes, fringed by thick black lashes, appear designed solely to see beauty in the world. An old ribbon adorns her curly locks and she wears an apricot-coloured threadbare dress. Yamina is used to walking on thorns, running over the bare earth and rushing down rocky slopes.

Rahma entrusts her daughter with simple household tasks. She considers her gifted and notices how surprisingly well-coordinated she is, for her age. Yamina is resourceful enough to be sent to fetch water by herself. She doesn't say much, or cry, and goes to sleep without complaining. She never brings shame on her mother.

She's a great child, this five-year-old, an animal lover who enjoys stroking the goats in the backyard. When the time comes to sell the calf, she clings to the beast's neck and weeps. She has always struggled when it comes to separations.

What fascinates young Yamina is counting the canopy of

stars above the douar. Every night, she points up at the sky as if trying to touch the stars. She does so until everything begins to spin.

During the summer months, sleeping in the yard to enjoy the coolness of the night was sweet compensation after spending the day working under the blazing sun.

But now it is ill-advised. French soldiers might raid the mechtas at any moment. Jeddi Ahmed, Yamina's grandfather, the last man left in the household, has put a stop to the women sleeping outdoors.

This elder, all skin and bones, represents little threat in the eyes of the colonial army.

One day as Jeddi Ahmed is cradling Moussa, Yamina's baby brother, born a few months earlier, the soldiers burst into the mechta. There are ten or so of them. Yamina stares at their berets, their outsize shoes, their glistening skin, their thick fatigues. She witnesses them kick the door open and make themselves at home. She sees how they stride about, gesturing brutally; she hears them speaking loudly, rummaging everywhere. When she stares at their weapons she feels terror in the pit of her stomach.

Yamina keeps a check on her mother's pale face. Rahma may be dazzled by the sun, but she does not flinch, rather her face hardens in the way that has become second nature for her. The little girl's aunts and grandfather stand next to Rahma, stoical, forming a row against the low wall in the courtyard. Yamina understands that she too must fall in line and is quick to join them, pressing herself against her mother, seeking out the heat of her thighs.

'What about your husbands?' roars the man who seems to be in charge. 'Where are your husbands?'

Franssa, each woman answers in turn, adopting the same tone of voice.

This irritates the officer, who picks up a hessian sack and nervously empties its load of charcoal into the middle of the room. As the soldiers are vacating the premises, one of them, the youngest, halts in front of Jeddi Ahmed and fixes Moussa with a long stare. The baby looks dazed in the arms of the old man. Without taking his eyes off him, the young soldier slowly reaches for his weapon and aims it at the infant's forehead.

The grandfather barely stiffens, his knowledge of these men telling him to avoid any sudden movements. Rahma stands motionless against the low wall, observing the scene, choking back a cry that would split the mountainside, a mother resisting the urge to hurl herself at the soldier, to sink her teeth into his neck until blood is drawn.

Jeddi Ahmed watches his daughter out of the corner of his eye and the power of his gaze makes her abandon any thoughts of rebellion.

'Please, no,' says the old man, trying to soften up the conscript, 'show some pity, he's just a baby.'

What the soldier sees in Moussa is future danger, a threat to his own life.

'A baby?' he says to Jeddi Ahmed. 'Yeah, right! A baby who'll grow up and turn into another armed bandit – a fellagha – fighting French rule!'

Eventually, he lowers his machine gun.

By some miracle, the young Frenchman has come to his senses.

As the convoy of jeeps pulls away, Rahma loses consciousness at the feet of Yamina, who calmly brings sugar water to revive her mother.

Yamina's childhood has come to an abrupt end.

IMPASSE SAINT-FRANÇOIS
PARIS (75018)
FRANCE, 2018

Imane is convinced her father still holds it against her. When Brahim takes a dim view of something, he isn't the type to come round easily.

Theirs is a special relationship. As the third daughter, the one just before the son, the one who *should have been* the son, Imane senses she's disappointed her father, *yet again*.

She turns her studio upside down, all twenty square metres of it, in search of her Bershka mom jeans, €19.90. She doesn't know what to wear this morning. The weather keeps changing. She could check the weather app on her iPhone, but that feels like a dirty habit, or she could simply stick her head out of the window, except who does that these days?

Imane has promised Yamina she'll join the family for Saturday lunch today. She's given them her word, and, in the Taleb family, you don't mess with your word. Imane knows she can't avoid home forever. She's already skipped two lunches, citing work commitments.

What she is avoiding, as everybody knows, is the look in Brahim's eyes.

Her father's gaze never lies, and although relations between them have improved over recent weeks, she can still read his disappointment – as familiar as it is excruciating – when their eyes lock. Imane has no idea how she held strong and went through with it. She felt like a feverish sparrow fleeing the nest while apologising for being able to fly.

'I'm thirty-one years old!' she kept repeating, clean out of arguments.

Yamina and Brahim don't consider being thirty-one a valid excuse. Why did their daughter want to leave the loving home where she was safe and cared for? To pay an excessive rent on a place she couldn't afford to heat properly in winter? To sleep alone? To drink her coffee standing in the kitchen? To do her own shopping and laundry?

What would people say?

Brahim's family has always enjoyed a good reputation. His wife is well-regarded. His children haven't turned out badly, which was not a given, considering the environment in which they were raised.

This family man has always been haunted by two fears. The first was the police beating down the front door at dawn to raid the apartment and arrest Omar. After all, it happened often enough around them. The second was one of his daughters losing her honour and bringing home a child conceived out of wedlock, a child Brahim wouldn't know what to do with and who would tarnish his honour.

When little else remains, honour matters.

Brahim is old these days and relieved to have escaped the worst. But ever since Imane left home he has been feeling anxious again. Daughters don't leave home before they're married, everyone knows that. Still, he opted for a strategy of trust, choosing to grant his children their freedom. He had always said that he didn't want to be like his own father, a cold and brutal man without a generous bone in his body. Brahim encouraged his children, never raising a hand against them and always urging them to study. All they could reproach him for was being poor and worn out by work.

When he takes stock, Brahim could have done much worse.

There's no denying he would have liked his son Omar to be made of tougher material. The boy's too sensitive, in his view. As a youngster, he didn't like to fight, he was quick to lose heart and the tears came easily.

As for his daughters, not one of them married, in the final count.

Well, Malika, the eldest, was married for a while.

A big fat celebration, like back in the home country.

Yes, she was young, but daughters *did* marry at eighteen in those days. It was 11 August 1999. The wedding invitations had been crudely cut out and cheesy motifs printed on the back: libidinous angels playing the harp in each corner of the card. The whole neighbourhood remembers the date because it was the day of the total eclipse of the sun. At the Avenir shopping centre in Drancy, they were handing out cardboard glasses meant to protect your eyes.

It was the dawn of the new millennium, and the eclipse offered a glimpse of the future.

When Yamina refers to her daughter's wedding, which isn't often, she is tongue-in-cheek about the eclipse: 'God sent us a clear sign! At the very moment when Malika said yes at the Mairie, one star hid another. Just like that, darkness! The message was clear for all to see! How could we have been so blind?'

Brahim danced at his daughter's wedding. His children and wife couldn't get over it, they'd never seen him dance before. Crossing and uncrossing his legs while sitting on his chair was the most graceful movement they had witnessed him perform in public.

They couldn't picture Brahim as a young man, dancing the twist in Paris in the sixties, wearing bell-bottomed trousers in the seventies and long hair in the eighties. And yet he, too, had straddled eras and fashions, just like everybody else.

But that was part of another story Brahim would never tell.

Encouraged by the Bedouin songs played on the flutes and bendir drums of the aarfa orchestra of Msirda, he had executed the traditional dance, shimmying with his shoulders while gripping the aassa, a sort of hand-carved wooden walking stick. When he did those up-down movements, he looked like he was digging, holding a spade, as if he were at work on the construction site. Perhaps it was only his wife who spotted, in the moment, the curious resemblance of their regional dance to her husband's work. The gestures were the same. Perhaps, without realising it, he had worn himself out his entire life by reproducing an ancient choreography on construction sites.

The way Brahim's heels struck the floor at his daughter's wedding was intense and skilful: *hup, hup, one, two, three… shoulders, shoulders, hup, one, two, three, four, five.* He was roaring with laughter, rejoicing like a man rewarded after years of sacrifices. Urged on by the clapping, Brahim, who wasn't yet known as 'Hajj' (the term of respect for those who have made their pilgrimage to Mecca, or else earned the moniker by dint of seniority) had well and truly danced.

Of course, not a trace of this final dance in public remains, the video of Malika's wedding having been smashed and thrown in the bin after the divorce. We think we can destroy memories by wiping cassettes and ripping up photos, but we don't get to choose when it comes to our memories, or Brahim would long ago have deleted this event from his own.

What he does remember is that his handsome moustache was still black, the year was pre-2000, and he paid the electricity bill by money order at the Bobigny Normandie Niemen office of EDF. Back then, Brahim was out and about every day with Père Ammouri, their neighbour, who was still alive.

Brahim felt foolish saying it, but the best always go first.

Kader Ammouri was like local royalty, a mascot. With his tall Berber physique, all lean and lanky, those big snaggle teeth inside a huge mouth forever telling his life story, he was a sort of Jacques Brel marinated in olive oil. He was the only person bold enough to use the informal *tu* when addressing the former mayor, Jack Ralite, and he did so without an ounce of embarrassment; the same went for holding his wife's hand in the street. This raised more than a few eyebrows and made ripples in the oued. They'd never seen anything like it before. A chibani, a white-haired elder, engaging in a public display of affection towards his woman. Well, that was enough to set the neighbourhood tongues wagging.

People couldn't begin to imagine just how soft Madame Ammouri's hands were, or how Tassadite, to those on first-name terms with her, felt like the Queen of Aubervilliers when she walked beside Kader.

Père Ammouri also translated paperwork for the other old men and accompanied them to claim their dues from the white bosses. He wasn't afraid of speaking loudly and raising his chin. He wasn't afraid of a fight either. Everybody remembers his legendary punch-up with the taxi driver he laid into one Saturday morning on the terrace of Le Chien qui Fume, the café opposite the Mairie.

Ah! Père Ammouri! He was a rare specimen. When he

attended Malika's wedding in August 1999 he still smoked like a trooper, without suspecting the cancer already nibbling at his throat.

The trouble is, it's not just his wife and children who miss him, it's not just Brahim who misses him, it's not just his friends who miss him, or the commune of Aubervilliers: Père Ammouri is the kind of man missed by the world.

There aren't many like him left. Unsurprisingly, they all clear off.

Yes, as Brahim Taleb has observed for some time now, everyone clears off. And yet he had felt so proud ... It was a visible sign of success, at last he was going to marry off his daughter. Even today, just thinking about it gives him twinges in his chest. It was a hard blow to take as a father. The first divorce in the family. *Divorce*. What sorrow to have to add this noisy, shame-laden word to the Talebs' dictionary.

Malika is his eldest daughter, and he holds himself responsible for her great misfortune. All these years on, he still feels guilty for *ruining her life*. In his mind, Malika is on the shelf.

He recalls the brides who were repudiated back in the village, sometimes the morning after their wedding night, for reasons undeclared, their families cast into disrepute, the women stripped of any chance of finding another husband.

Divorce is a scourge, in his eyes, a kind of death *for women*, although, and this hardly needs spelling out, *only for women*. Women die so many small deaths before the final one.

Brahim is of a generation that doesn't notice how men enjoy the privilege of dying just the once.

Women are murdered by their own world, a thousand times over. Yet still they rise again, morning after morning.

For a long time he dreamed about trussing up his son-in-law, stowing him in the boot of his red Citroën AX, driving to Georges Valbon County Park in la Courneuve, leaving the car at the Parking Tapis Vert, and carrying him on his back as far as the woods, in the higher reaches, sheltered from prying eyes. There, he strung him up by his feet and beat him black and blue, pummelling him with all his might, deploying his former builder's fists. At some point the dangling body swung from right to left, inanimate, prompting Brahim to come to his senses and abandon the corpse, without bothering to hide the traces of his crime.

It was an image, no more, but it haunted his nights.

His son-in-law was simply a youth of the times. He wasn't a Man according to Brahim's criteria. No Robert Mitchum or Lino Ventura. More to the point, he had a white girlfriend, Cassandra, who came to knock on Malika's door one morning with his child in her arms. The son-in-law had an illegitimate family and Malika, with the innocence of her eighteen years, wept for hours while listening to her Boyz II Men cassette before she could face telling her mother. Malika didn't love her husband any more than her husband loved her.

They hadn't chosen one another.

After just a few months of marriage, Malika started to feel lonely, while her husband loitered in the café, playing scratch cards, his thumbnails turning completely grey.

And yet the arrangement between the fathers, who had a mutual appreciation for one another, had come about so smoothly. The two men agreed on everything. Their children, who had barely spoken barring the odd occasion, politely consented to marry one another.

The first time, Yamina held out the telephone to Malika who shrugged off her Walkman headphones. She seemed put out at having to pause her excellent Zouk Love mixtape, and snatched the receiver while her mother urged in a fake whisper: 'Here you are, my daughter, it's your fiancé!'

Yamina pretended to leave the room to afford them more privacy, but hovered on the threshold, leaning against the door, arms folded, face beaming.

Malika was left staring awkwardly at the big fat buttons on the telephone, which rested on a handmade lace doily. 'Helloooooo,' she said to the person at the other end, pointlessly stretching out the last syllable, and prompting Yamina to give her eldest daughter an absurd thumbs-up by way of encouragement. The young couple briefly exchanged small talk, and then, without further ado, Malika hung up. She put her headphones back on and closed her eyes, swaying her head to the Tony Deloumeaux song 'L'Anmou an Kado'.

Malika's real love was creole band music.

She still remembers her fiancé asking if she knew how to cook, and that she responded like a dolt, drawing up a list of her most accomplished dishes. Back then, she hadn't read *King Kong Theory* by Virginie Despentes or listened to hundreds of feminist podcasts; no, back in the day, Malika was content to tread a well-worn path, and nobody can hold that against her.

It happened *the way it was supposed to*. There was no precedent. Malika was the first Taleb daughter to get married. No more, no less.

Her only role model was Tata Norah, her young auntie in Algeria. Malika remembered Norah's head sinking beneath the weight of the ritual chedda – the bridal headdress of Tlemcen – and, later on, in the house of Norah's husband, an older woman flapping a bloodstained sheet. Malika was twelve at the time and thought Norah had just been murdered.

The firstborn children, like Malika, knew their parents were only doing their best, which explains why they fell in with these outmoded rules. After all, rules of some kind were necessary, hence their creation. Perhaps these families were only passing through, perhaps they still believed in a miraculous return, but they still needed to be organised.

Even a temporary life requires order. Which accounts for their hybrid laws, invented instinctively at a crossroads between the village of their recollections and their notion of *here*.

Because they were living *here*. And it was time to admit this. True, they hadn't expected to be here this long. This country has a gift for robbing people of their years, a flair for confiscating their hopes and burying their dreams in thousands of tiny coffins.

No one notices time slipping by until, one fine day, the children are grown up and you're calculating your pension credits. Making the right choices isn't easy when you don't understand the codes. They worried about losing everything, about jeopardising their futures, so they clung on to *who they were*. They didn't want to renounce their identity. *They refused to be erased, AGAIN. How could they not fear erasure?* It's what this country did best, it had already tried to erase them, the first generation, and now it was targeting their children.

Brahim reflected on this sometimes when he was using white spirit. It struck him that France was erasing them, much as this solvent removed undesirable stains. Had Brahim been able to speak English, he would have been stunned to discover what the name meant.

Malika was too young to suggest other options. She missed out on the good fortune enjoyed by her younger sisters,

Imane and Hannah. More's the pity, because within a few years she could have chosen the life she wanted. Such is the eldest daughter's lot. Not that she holds this against Yamina and Brahim, she was their queen, after all, and they cherished her, so she could hardly complain. Like many children of her generation, she resigned herself to what happened and forgave her parents for being out of touch with reality.

Looking back on it today, she tells herself: *They did what seemed right to them at the time.*

Brahim blames himself enough as it is. He is convinced his two other daughters didn't want to marry because of *the Malika mess-up.*

And it's true that, ever since, neither of them has found men on a par.

On a par with Brahim.

'Do you want to kill your father?' was Yamina's response on the day that Imane dared float the idea of moving into a studio flat.

Her youngest daughter sighed, albeit behind her mother's back, so as not to show any disrespect. Living in Drama Land was heavy going.

Imane is thirty-one and ashamed. She doesn't consider her struggles to be age-appropriate. Her parents make her feel she'll be sixteen forever. In her efforts not to hurt them, Imane has been making half-baked decisions, running scared and steering clear of love. It's time to 'fess up to this half-life she's been leading on their behalf, whereby she's too afraid to stand up to them or make them accept her choices.

This Saturday, Yamina has prepared loubia djej for lunch: white beans with chicken is one of Imane's favourites. Brahim has enquired after his children's work, showing each of them the same interest, affording them the same consideration.

And there was Imane working herself up into a state about it, fearing an accusation of betrayal where there was only mild concern. The prospect of disappointing them mortifies her.

To disappoint parents like hers would be horrific, the worst thing she could do.

They've made so many sacrifices.

Crushing sacrifices.

And yet, despite all their efforts to the contrary, they've ended up raising overburdened children.

No shortage of towns and cities with kids like that, and they're easy enough to spot: overburdened children walk just like their parents do, heads down.

COMMUNE OF AHFIR
PROVINCE OF BERKANE
MOROCCO, 1956

They had left Algeria.

And it was like saying farewell to a mother.

This was the first exile.

The genesis of a life like a tug-of-war.

The family set off by mule after the dawn prayer. Rahma's satchel contained a loaf of rye bread, some water, a little sugar and two raw onions.

They left nothing behind that mattered, apart from their story, strips of their flesh and a few ghosts, thousands of ghosts perhaps. It was too early to count.

Yamina was still drowsy. It was cold, and in the distance, they could hear the howling of the golden jackals. The little girl pretended she wasn't afraid. She had learned early on to stifle her emotions. As the family convoy headed off, the clay house of Yamina's birth kept shrinking until it vanished behind the cactuses.

There was the fig tree too, the one she had climbed more times than she could remember, imploring, it seemed to her, to be taken with them. But Yamina already knew what happened when you uprooted a tree.

Jeddi Ahmed wiped his teary eyes in his razza, his yellow satin turban. Every gesture pained him. The old man's skinny hands had built so much in their time, though you wouldn't have bet on it when you saw them trembling. The war, their hunger, this journey – it felt like a curse, the lot of heroes in ancient tales, as told to children in the villages after nightfall.

Once they were on the other side, in Morocco, Yamina could have sworn they were still in Msirda. Nothing struck her as different. Except that here they were no longer at home.

Here, Yamina no longer dared to climb trees.

The family had moved in with Rahma's mother who welcomed them into her modest house where everybody slept in the same room. The village, Ahfir, bore a Berber name meaning 'holes'. It can never be overstated how much the names of places and objects matter.

The fact they had arrived here to be swallowed up by holes, and for the years to drag on interminably, was no coincidence. This was only the start of their run of miserable luck.

Yamina's father was away at the front. She had almost

forgotten his face. Sometimes, she could conjure his blue eyes for the briefest moment. Only then would she feel soothed. What a handsome man! Yamina had never laid eyes on a finer face than her father's. His gaze, his shoulders, his long legs and his proud brow were unequivocally in harmony. He had arrived in this world to become a hero. He had the looks *and* the guts.

Yamina used to tell the little girls in the street that her father could liberate a whole country, single-handed, and also that he was brave enough, single-handed, to help an entire people rise up. Any girl who dared call her a liar was in for a memorable licking. Sometimes Yamina picked a fight with the little Moroccan girls on the way to the madrasa, becoming blind, losing all self-control, which had never happened before. She kept on hitting until the other girl was awash with tears, or blood, or else had wet herself; and she only relaxed her grip if the offender had paid the price, if she was ashamed, if she was pleading with Yamina to let her go. The girl had to beg for forgiveness, down on her knees. Only then would Yamina come to her senses.

Such violence was new to the little girl's body. She was afraid of the blinding heat that coursed through her limbs. And yet, no matter the beating her mother doled out, she flared up again the moment the opportunity arose. 'What's got into you? What's made you so hard?'

Crouched in a corner of the dilapidated room, on a hot

afternoon, she watches her mother who, having dispensed a blistering hiding, returns to her sewing. She is sewing flags. Green, white and red.

Each flag sewn by Rahma from scraps of salvaged fabric represents the hope that one day she will wave it proudly above her head, in the direction of a merciful sky. This day will come, soon.

Yamina never wearies of her mother's handiwork, of her slender and delicate hands, index finger against thumb, her three other fingers in the air. As she pulls the needle upwards, then pushes it back down again to pierce the fabric, she combines the elegance of an orchestra conductor with the grace of an Egyptian dancer.

Rahma promises her children they will soon return to their country, where they will be able to see their house again and live in peace. 'And the fig tree?' Yamina keeps asking. 'Will the fig tree still be there?'

During this period other children are added to the list of mouths to feed: two of Yamina's brothers are born in exile. Mohamed Madouri, the father of the family, miraculously reappears now and then, on leave from the front. He doesn't stay long, a few days at most, just long enough to receive new instructions. Above all, he lets them know that he is alive and liberation is within reach.

But Mohamed Madouri does not kiss his daughter or take her in his arms. Only this, before leaving again: he puts his hands on her shoulders and stares at her. Yamina stares back and tries to fathom those eyes, interpreting his heavy stares as a sign of encouragement, an exhortation to stay upright. In those exchanges of looks, she feels as important as any son.

Mohamed Madouri wanted his children to learn to read.

This was what he had retained from his years in Paris: in trains, in parks, on café terraces, everywhere, people reading books. He, the lonely native, born in the town of Boukanoun, north of Ahfir, the illiterate shepherd who abandoned his goats on their mountainside to seek his meagre fortune in the Metropole, would watch these women absorbed by their books, observe them licking the tip of their index finger to turn the page, and he was fascinated.

It was probably too late for him, but one day he would have children, and he vowed they would learn to read.

When the time came for him to return, he had not forgotten. The country would soon be independent, and the first free generation needed to be educated.

And so Yamina goes to the madrasa, as one of the few girls to attend the Quranic school of Ahfir. She sets off with her little brother Moussa, while the village is still plunged in darkness. The fqih, their near-deaf elderly teacher, is strict with them. There is a wooden board on which the children write, with the help of a bamboo stick split in two at the tip. Even today, Yamina can still recall how they burned wool; and how, by adding a little water to the harvested ashes, they produced ink.

Tirelessly, they wrote out verses on the board, and if they hadn't memorised them perfectly, they had to start all over again. Yamina has always understood that learning requires pain and effort.

Sometimes, in the middle of the night, secret meetings take place in her grandmother's house in Ahfir.

Yamina crouches down and listens in, ears to the wall, resulting in traces of limewash on her blue shirt which was rescued from the stinking Red Cross bundles on a day of provisioning or '*pro'vizz*'. For the children of Algerian refugees, days of supplies are better than any celebration.

Women who are strangers issue instructions: 'Don't argue, be discreet, don't draw any attention to yourselves. Make sure your children are well-behaved, be good neighbours, don't talk about your husbands, don't talk about your brothers, say nothing about the war, nothing about the actions of the combatants, remain invisible.'

Hearing these words, Yamina senses that *remaining invisible* is a matter of survival.

She will always know the overwhelming sorrow of those who feel as if they have left everything behind, when they possessed nothing in the first place.

She will always know the terrible illusion of thinking you can leave a place, return there, and find things just as you left them.

BRASSERIE LE COQ FRANÇAIS, RUE DE PARIS
LES LILAS (93260)
FRANCE, 2019

Hannah arrives early for her date.

She is ahead of schedule, same as always.

A premature baby. Then a precocious child. And, finally, an indignant grown-up. Always quicker to notice something than anyone else.

She knows that it's a punishing way to live your life. At thirty-four, she feels worn out.

He's not much of a looker, this guy: bit of a paunch, hairy fingers, hopelessly small eyes and a habit of cutting her off mid-flow. Last time he interrupted her every sentence with his stupid remarks. He wastes words, makes embarrassing attempts at jokes and wears aftershave that's too floral to be masculine.

The lack of masculinity is a real problem for Hannah.

Still, she had decided to make an effort this time. Be less drastic, give the product a chance. It was their second date, and she was willing to overlook the fact he was wearing slim bootcut jeans that were too snug around the hips.

Yes, *hip-hugging*.

If Hannah notices the *hips* of a man, he automatically becomes a sister, and she's not looking for another sister.

Hakim shows up on the café terrace, all smiles and curvy hips. Hannah watches him wend his way between the tables. *He moves like the star belly dancer at some Moroccan restaurant in the provinces.*

She sighs.

From her perspective, all this guy has going for him is his ambition. Which is a rarity: straightforward, unalloyed ambition, nothing showy about it, nothing dodgy either, just the classic story of the self-made man.

Hakim set up his first business at twenty-four, providing cleaning services as a subcontractor. He employs women to clean the offices of small and medium-sized businesses in the banlieue: suburban SMEs. Plus, he recently launched an organic halal sandwich shop, and business is booming. He's not short of money, which gives him an above-average opinion of himself.

The one time an Arab shows some interest in me...

Usually, when they've achieved a degree of social success, Arab boys like to strut their stuff on the arms of white women, as the ultimate and irrefutable proof of their triumph. And sometimes they take it further. Going around saying they're not into Arab girls, that they won't even consider them. They claim it'd be like incest. Spout nonsense about *familiarity killing desire*. But they don't marry Black girls instead. Hell, no!

In the successful integration league, the straight-haired white woman represents the cherry on the cake. These men will accept in a white woman what they'd never stand for in an Arab girl. For everything they'd forbid their sister, they've already signed a waiver clause with their white girlfriend. She can be less educated, dim and with an average body, but she'll still be worth ten points more in their eyes. Of course, they'll make out it's love, the real deal, pure and simple. Who says love gets a free pass when it comes to social conditioning?

Hannah distrusts anyone who suffers from hatred of their own kind. She can find no excuse, she judges them mercilessly, bears a grudge. She thinks they're behind the curve, they haven't understood anything, they're slaves in the colonial hierarchy, worse than their parents. Worse, because their parents couldn't have known.

Hannah thinks Arab boys seeking this kind of erasure are like lumps of sugar in hot coffee.

To cap it all, they reckon they're emancipated.

Mainly, Hannah hates people who hate themselves. She can spot the Arab boys in that category straight off, and occasionally feels the urge to say to them: 'You're idiots. You're holding us back. You're the greatest obstacle in our struggle.' So, anyway, this time, and it doesn't happen often, Hannah has an Arab who's interested in her.

It's not like she hasn't tried. She even fell in love once or twice, a few years back.

There was one boyfriend, in particular. But their relationship never took off. He felt threatened by Hannah's strong personality. Scared she'd take over, he lived in permanent fear of being dominated, of her sinking her teeth into him, chewing and swallowing. So, he started trying to control her and that got her back up: 'Listen! Not even my own father forbids me from doing stuff, so what gives you the right?' But she ended up feeling a fool. *Fuck's sake, Papa's got nothing to do with this, what am I doing bringing him into it?*

He was called Sami and, at over thirty, he wore a baseball cap summer and winter. Shame, given he was funny and creative, but he hadn't received enough love to know how to give it back. They parted on bad terms, with Hannah ditching Sami and feeling blue about it for a long time afterwards. But she got over her heartbreak, in the end.

Then one day she found out he had died in a road accident.

She recalled his laugh, his habit of holding the steering wheel in one hand, the first time he'd told her: 'I love you,' in front of the UGC cinema in Rosny after they'd watched a romcom with Hilary Swank. The film bored the pants off her, from what Hannah recalls, plus Swank's jutting jawline bugged her throughout, but, against all odds, Sami was moved to tears, and on their way back to the car he grabbed her by the waist and said: 'I love you,' looking straight into her eyes. She didn't know what to say and that vexed him. It was a big deal for him, because he'd never said those words to anyone before her. It was a first for Hannah too, no one had ever uttered those words to her. The drive home, in the 2004 black Volkswagen Polo, was awkward with both of them pretending nothing had happened. Sami turned on the radio and it was Skyrock's night-time phone-in, with male pundits cotching crudely about sex. It was embarrassing, but not as bad as talking about real emotions.

Hakim, the entrepreneur with the chubster hips, talks about himself while drinking his café allongé, *me, me, me,* and Hannah does her best to stay focused. But she can feel her mind slipping away as she watches his big fat pink lips moving.

Hannah, who quickly tires of things, of people, struggles with this, and it's no picnic feeling bored with life. You're forever having to reinvent your existence. Everything has to be intense for her, all the time, or there's no point.

Hakim is talking about his musical tastes, and she'd put a million dollars on him saying: 'I love funk, it's all I listen to.' She wants to yell in his face: 'Fuck's sake, surprise me, why don't you? Of course you love funk, you're a forty-three-year-old man of Moroccan heritage from the banlieue!'

The moment he said his best trip ever was to Thailand, she zoned out for good. As for originality, let's not go there.

Hannah had already guessed it all, down to the tiniest detail.

They set off like so many – a bunch of five or six guys from the endz. It was the early noughties, the summer of 2001 to be precise, 'Hey, those were good times,' just before 9/11, before bin Laden, before *Charlie Hebdo*. When Arabs were flavour of the month, thanks to Zidane and his two goals in the 1998 World Cup final, the jokes of Jamel Debbouze, and Rachid Arhab presenting the one o'clock news on France 2. It was cool to be 'rebeu' back then. (*Arabe* flipped via backslang to second generation *beur*, and on again to *rebeu*.)

This period only lasted three or four years, but Hakim and his bredrin made the most of it.

They were super-excited about the exotic destination. Hakim was gearing up to make a dream come true: going on holiday somewhere that wasn't Morocco for the first time in his life, and without his parents too.

Before they set off, he treated himself to a top-notch fade haircut over at Ali Coiffure, Ali being *the ace of the 1-cut*. Hakim even dared to bleach his hair baby-chick yellow. He wore the perfect outfit for the kid from the banlieue, summer 2000, millennium style: Com8 T-shirt, fake Cartier sunglasses, Azzaro's Chrome pour homme, Lacoste bag, bling in his ear, and a neck chain with silver coffee beans.

He often revisited that trip as the highpoint of his youth, maybe his life.

He probably bought a cargo-load of Versace men's underpants at the MBK Center in Bangkok, nice price, 100 baht a pair.

How could he forget the Thai boxing match he attended with his boys at the Lumpini Stadium? The atmosphere was on fire! It made him want to take up the sport but one of his friends dissuaded him: 'My bredrin, wallah, you're not fit for it. Like, don't take this the wrong way, yeah, but you're a chubster, you get me, you got man boobs, bro.'

So, Hakim gave up on the idea of buying a pair of satin Thai boxing shorts, in a special black and gold edition. Not that they had any left in XL.

Nor did he escape the inevitable photo at Tiger Kingdom, where he can be seen bottle-feeding a tiger cub too docile not to be drugged.

Hakim was more romantic than he appeared and, at twenty, he was ready to fall in love with the first woman he met. In Patong, he found Sumalee, the girl with pink cheeks and English as hopeless as Hakim's. She was sweet and kind, and some evenings he still dreams of her brown eyes. It seemed to him that they were sharing a special moment together, the beginning of a love story, above and beyond the traditional massage option plus Happy Ending.

After visiting the same massage parlour on three consecutive evenings and parting with more than 2,500 baht, one of his friends – the same one who'd convinced him not to take up a career in Muay Thai boxing on account of his flab – tried to stop Hakim from returning a fourth time: 'Wallah, my bredrin, I'm smelling trouble, is she like some Thai-style marabout or what, doing her witchcraft on you? Belek, bro, gotta be on your guard, you get me, I think you're falling in love, my bredrin.'

Hakim left his best memories behind in Thailand, along with his virginity and a wad of cash. A trip like that, in his twenties, was the ultimate initiation rite for boys like him.

Thailand had made men of them.

If wearing slim bootcut jeans, snug around the hips, constitutes being a man.

Too bad for Hannah.

At least, for once, she had sparked an Arab boy's interest.

MARKET ON BOULEVARD DE OUJDA
COMMUNE OF AHFIR, PROVINCE OF BERKANE
MOROCCO, 1959

We're in the heart of Souk Ahfir, on boulevard de Oujda.

A crowd is already rubbing shoulders at the popular market. Onlookers jostle, intent on filling their wicker baskets with meagre provisions.

Women queue up for the communal oven with enormous trays on their heads as they wait to hand over their loaves for baking. The pleasing aroma of freshly made biscuits fills the air.

Small boys with blackened hands wax the shoes of those they take for 'big men', while frightened fowl flap their wings in cages on the ground, preparing for their destiny.

And then there are the other kids, the ones who beg.

Yamina wends her way through the throng, protecting her swollen cheek with her tiny hand and zigzagging between the elbows of passers-by.

Her gaze meets that of a young girl, scarcely older than she is, begging, and whom Yamina witnesses clutching at men's arms, tugging on women's djellabas, muttering and pleading with them, only to be cast off. The market folk ignore her, not one of them stops to give her a coin or a hunk of bread, they can't even spare a kind word. Everybody in this place is famished, or else nobody has any pity.

Yamina feels the beggar girl's sorrow.

Even though this toothache is making her head spin, she tells herself that even if she had a date or a carrot, she would share it with her. What she can do is to go over and stroke the girl's shoulder before carrying on her way.

Yamina could never hold out her hands to beg. Her father would rather see his kids starve to death than let them become street urchins.

She has been suffering from a raging toothache for several days. Only when it became unbearable did Rahma make up her mind to send her daughter to the *tooth puller*. Yamina has just turned ten.

The man, who has no qualifications, no medical expertise whatsoever, receives her in the heart of Souk Ahfir, inside his improvised consulting room: a green tent, erected between the soap seller's stall and the cobbler's canvas. He is known for practising hijama – the wet-cupping of ancestral prophetic medicine – and is responsible for circumcising the village boys. He also sells chemical powders for the home to exterminate insects and rats. Yamina stares at the boxes piled up in front of her and the terrifying pictures of red-eyed rats.

When the cantankerous tooth puller orders her to sit down on a wooden stall and open her mouth, she barely has time to glance at his tools. In truth, he has just the one small pair of blacksmiths pliers, unsterilised.

It's worse than the darkest nightmare.

The man pulls out her tooth with such violence that it makes an appalling sound, one which Yamina will never forget. The tooth, still caught in the pliers and under pressure from the tooth puller's grip, crumbles.

Yamina cries out, her head about to explode, blood oozing inside her throat. The voices, the rumble, the maddening roar of the market: everything begins to fade. Yamina's vision blurs and she can feel herself slipping away. Never has she experienced such pain.

The tooth puller doesn't give her any time to gather her wits, doesn't offer her a scrap of cloth or a wad of cotton. She is crying and unsteady on her feet, but he immediately demands the coins she owes him, then sends her packing. 'Once you're home, rinse your mouth out with salt water,' he tells her, wiping his hands on his canvas trousers.

Yamina must now walk back on her own, beneath a scalding sun, to reach the house.

For the next fourteen years, until 1973, she will suffer

regularly from abscesses and migraines, and nobody will show the slightest concern.

One day, in desperation, unable to bear the pain any longer, she will peer into a pocket mirror and gouge her bleeding gum with a vine stem, until, at last, she extracts a large black fragment. The chunk of tooth forgotten by the tooth puller.

COMMUNE OF AUBERVILLIERS
DEPARTMENT OF SEINE–SAINT–DENIS (93300)
FRANCE, 2019

Yamina wakes at dawn, as she does every morning.

She has one of those automatic Azan alarm clocks that calls her to prayer. Hannah ordered it on alhidayah.fr. A thoughtful daughter, she frequently gives small presents like this to her mother, who thanks her each time with: 'You shouldn't have. Keep your money for yourself, binti.'

There's a choice of more than a thousand towns in the settings menu. The first time she used the clock, Yamina put her reading glasses and searched the list for Aubervilliers, but to no avail. So she ended up selecting Paris on the rebound. Next, she clicked on Muezzin, and chose her favourite reciter: Abdul Rahman Al Sudais. When she subscribed to Iqraa TV, she used to listen to his sermons in Mecca every Friday. Her children would watch her, knowing it was only a matter of time. Yamina always ended up in tears. She's filled with faith, Yamina. In secret, the Taleb children are saving up so that one day she can perform Hajj.

As she makes her way soundlessly towards the bathroom, for her ablutions, she remembers she had that dream again, last night.

She must be very young. She's wearing her schoolgirl's apron, struggling to make it to class on time, down the village slope with her old clodhoppers and the small satchel on her back. The sun pierces the clouds and Yamina feels blessed. She enjoys school and is the best student in the area. The headmaster often holds her up as an example. Yamina is brilliant, quick to learn. But as she arrives at the small building, the gates close in front of her. She can't go inside. She starts shouting and banging. 'Let me in, I want to come in! Let me in to school! I want to study!'

Her father appears, his face pale under the big hood of his brown djellaba, and he frowns as he takes his little girl by the arm, dragging her back home.

It's exactly fifty-seven years since Yamina was forced to leave school, to help her parents on the farm and to raise her brothers and sisters.

Five of her six brothers became teachers, and one an insurance agent.

As for Yamina, even at seventy she still wears a satchel in her dreams.

COMMUNE OF AHFIR
PROVINCE OF BERKANE
MOROCCO, JULY 1962

It was time to fly the flags.

The news came first to Dar el Jeb'ha, the house on the frontline, before spreading through all the houses like a great fire. Algeria was free.

Yamina will never forget the excitement: the entire street dancing, women parading, making their youyou, chanting 'Tahia el Djazaïr!' – 'Long live Algeria!' – their white hayeks waltzing in the July sunlight.

For the parade, Yamina wore an outfit in the country's colours, designed by Rahma: green skirt, white blouse and red neckerchief. She had never seen her mother so elated. Rahma kept kissing her eldest daughter on the head, cheeks and hands, overflowing with joy and affection. It was miraculous, and so was this liberation of a country, the jubilation of a people rising up.

Ordinarily, Rahma was cold to the point of being inaccessible, locked off. But for all that the mother was uncomfortable when it came to physical contact, even with her own children, Yamina never held this against her. The daughter understanding that making a show of affection was no proof of it.

Our feelings require room to express themselves, and the trouble with war and poverty is that they occupy all the space.

Yamina was used to keeping herself in check, like her mother, her emotions trapped inside her tense young body. The body doesn't always cooperate with the heart, so that even when the heart blazes and rejoices, the body can remain stiff and awkward. Sometimes, heart and body become strangers to one another, no longer fluent in the same language. But Yamina seized on this rare occasion with the greed of a child deprived of tenderness, relishing her mother's gestures.

Rahma held her newest born in her arms, Djamila, named in honour of Djamila Bouhired, heroine of the Algerian resistance and a woman who would prove an enduring role model for Yamina, a figure of courage and dignity.

Having joined the struggle at nineteen, she was the emancipated big sister Yamina had always dreamed of. For a twelve-year-old girl, impatient to see her fig tree again, not only was Djamila Bouhired a symbol of the freedom struggle in Algeria, Djamila Bouhired *was* Algeria.

Many years later, Yamina would take with her to France a newspaper photo cut out of the pages of *Liberté* showing

Djamila, resplendent in her white corolla dress, on an official visit to Egypt, shaking the hand of an enthralled President Nasser.

The time had come for Yamina to find out what had happened to her fig tree.

COMMUNE OF AUBERVILLIERS
DEPARTMENT OF SEINE–SAINT–DENIS (93300)
FRANCE, 2019

Omar has never been *that kind* of brother.

He has never remarked on how his sisters dress, the company they keep or what time of night they make it home. He doesn't consider he has anything to say on the subject, especially given they're all older than him. Imane, Hannah and Malika are like three little mothers for Omar.

He has grown up in the company of women.

Omar's sisters have three dramatically different personalities. Their father calls them morning, noon and night, and it makes him chuckle. 'Ah, my daughters, are like medicine!' Brahim likes to say. 'It's morning, noon and night with them!'

As for Omar, he has the makings of a caricature, although by some miracle he hasn't become one.

The lastborn, the darling brown-eyed boy, the prodigal son, Maman's baby. Omar looked set to become an egocentric tyrant. And even though Yamina flatly denies it, her heart has tilted in a certain direction since Omar's birth. 'My daughter,' she's been known to admonish Hannah, 'stand up, that's your brother's place!'

In real life, finding *his* place hasn't proved so easy.

Omar never had much practice.

He was born on a throne. But out in the big wide world he'll never be king.

Omar has never scalded his lips on hot milk.

His mother always takes care to cool it for him, decanting it from one glass to another until it reaches the ideal temperature. To this day, she continues to dip her little finger in it, to make sure. She does so discreetly, safe from Hannah's thunderous gaze.

'Wallah, Maman, hel-lo, he's twenty-nine for goodness' sake!' Hannah explodes if she catches her mother red-handed. 'You're taking it too far. Where are we going with this? Look at him! He's got a beard, right? So let him fend for himself! I bet Gaddafi didn't have someone to blow on his milk!'

Yamina spares a thought for Gaddafi, his capture, the way he was beaten all over, dragged along the ground like a dog in agony, his face swollen and bloodied, and she is filled with compassion. At the time, she couldn't watch the footage to the end. She was imagining not only Gaddafi's pain but also, and above all, the pain of Gaddafi's mother. Nobody spared a thought for that poor woman, *meskina*, or what she endured.

Malika, the eldest, observes the relationship between

mother and son from a distance.

'Apparently Amin Maalouf wrote: "Misogyny is handed down from mother to daughter."'

Whenever Malika quotes an author, she prefaces it with *apparently,* which weakens the credibility of her argument, despite the quotation being spot on. For all that she over-intellectualises, most of her theories hold up: 'When we give birth to sons, we reproduce our own experiences as women. We differentiate according to gender, we value boys more, we reproduce the diktats of the patriarchy without realising it, and sometimes we do so more ferociously. You see how natural it is for Maman? She's internalised everything. We're making our own monsters. Just like in *Frankenstein.*'

The nod to *Frankenstein* tickles Hannah. 'Too right we are! Let's call him "Omarenstein"!'

They laugh in Omar's face and beard.

His sisters' remarks bounce off Omar: he is far from deluded, and tends to agree with the theories of Malika, Amin Maalouf and anyone else who speaks truth to this shitty society.

But the subtle process by which misogyny is internalised escapes Yamina.

'All that because I blew on his hot milk? My son's not a monster! Drink, my son. Don't listen to them!'

'Inshallah I don't have any children, because if it's just to treat them differently, what's the point?' asks Imane, aloof, raising her eyebrows.

'Nonsense, I don't treat them differently, my children are like the fingers on my hands – I can't just cut one of them off.'

Convinced she's Yamina's little finger, the one without any purpose, Imane leaves the room.

Yamina has been known to give her husband the cold shoulder if he forgets to buy more cereal for Omar's breakfast. Coco Pops. Her son's favourite. Below the expiry date, boxes of Coco Pops should have an age limit stamped on them.

'Chill, Maman!' insists Hannah, who has fuelled her own exasperation for years. 'We're out of cereal, so what's the big deal? It's not like we're going to hold a minute's silence!'

The last spontaneous minute's silence in the Taleb household occurred on 6 October 2001, a black day for French Algerians of Yamina's children's generation.

The friendly match between France and Algeria – and the first played between these two sides since Algerian independence – descended into chaos.

After booing the Marseillaise, fans ended up invading the pitch, and a few blissed-out bare-chested idiots spoiled the party for all concerned. How ironic that they sabotaged everything not with violence but with smiles, because they were happy to be there, to exist, at last.

Brahim switched off the television when Marie-George

Buffet, Minister of Youth Affairs and Sports, intervened in what was probably the most embarrassing low point. Omar remembers she sounded like a teacher shouting at a group of fourteen-to-sixteen-year-olds at risk of being excluded. 'You're better than this! Hel-lo? Can we all remember how to behave, please? Shh… pipe down, that's enough now! I'm warning you, if you don't stop, I'll have to cancel our Go Ape trip.'

She was this close to cutting their Coco Pops rations.

It's true that Omar has never gone hungry. God knows how, but Yamina always sets something aside, just in case. Even when he's working nights and returns home at dawn, her son is guaranteed to find a plate in the fridge covered in umpteen layers of clingfilm. He can guess at the chicken casserole, slow-cooked lamb or vegetable lasagne underneath. He eats in his bedroom, where nothing beats dunking his mother's homemade flatbread (the world's best matlou) in saffron-scented sauce at five in the morning.

Meanwhile, lying on her side in the bedroom at the rear of the apartment, Yamina, woken by some instinct, has had her eyes open in the dark for some time.

It's always the same rigmarole: tracing her son's journey in her head, guessing when he'll switch off the app, estimating how long the return trip will take him, trying not to think about the overloaded heavy goods vehicles speeding on the A1, then counting his steps from the Renault Talisman, which he always parks in the same place, under the street lamp in front of Chez Akfadou, the halal butcher run by Kabyles, opposite the gas-powered rotisserie (thirty-four chicken capacity).

Yamina pictures his haggard face. *My poor boy, how hard he works, what a plucky kid.* When she hears the clink of the key in the lock, her heart finally relaxes, reassured that nothing has happened to her son. Taxi driving is a dangerous profession, especially for a mother with an overactive imagination. Only then can she drift back to sleep, serene and proud.

She has made some progress: she no longer gets up to open the door for him or to warm his food. Abiding by Omar's request that she stay in bed requires no small effort.

Not that it stops there.

She still cleans his shoes, brews hot thyme infusions at the first sign of a cough, tidies his bedroom and wrestles with the urge to call him on the phone when he has passengers in the car.

Omar's clothes are always impeccably ironed, and when he puts on his shirt the waft of lavender makes him feel like he's walking on air. His mother tries to make Omar's life as soft and gentle as a washing detergent advert.

Sadly, real life doesn't match the soap suds ads.

In real life you find creases, sweat and grime, and you'd better be ready for them.

COMMUNE OF ARBOUZE

PROVINCE OF MSIRDA FOUAGA

ALGERIA, 1963

Yamina crouches down at the foot of the dead fig tree and stays there a while, feeling wretched.

Her beautiful fig tree won't come into bud again.

This girl, just shy of fourteen, looks ten or eleven at most: she and her brothers have experienced years of malnourishment. She rests her frail hands on the trunk of her childhood tree.

How will she tell her mother that Sid Ahmed, the grocer, has categorically refused to put their goods on tick? 'Your father's slate is too full! You'll have to pay me first! Go home!' His harsh rebuke in front of the other customers made Yamina look down at the ground and her cheeks stream with tears. And so, with a heavy heart and a dismayingly empty basket, she turned away, knowing she would have to find the courage to walk all those kilometres back to the house.

It's exhausting to return home defeated.

Rahma is waiting for her on the threshold, hand on hip.

'Well? Where's the shopping?'

Behind her, the other children bawl their hunger.

Yamina's eyes tell the whole story as she walks in empty-handed.

It doesn't occur to Rahma to comfort her daughter, nor does she acknowledge the humiliation inflicted by the grocer. She is furious, shooting Yamina a dark look and ripping the basket out of the hands of her firstborn.

'It's your fault! You don't know how to talk! You're good for nothing! Always looking at the ground! What are we going to do now? Who will feed your brothers? Eh? And what about your father? What's he going to say? He'll kill us!'

Mohamed Madouri has gone from independence hero to dominoes champion, roaming the area in search of makeshift jobs, trying to get by. Or else he loiters at the café, playing cards and smoking bad tobacco. He is obsessive and constantly out of sorts. His temper comes crashing down on Rahma, should she be rash enough to complain.

Yamina hates it when her father turns violent. She detests intervening between her mother and him, taking the blows herself, no longer recognising the look in his eyes, which is normally so gentle. The war has robbed Mohamed Madouri of his kindness as well as his calm.

There is no work. The land is parched. The countrymen have lost everything. Some are unable to recover their land because they no longer bear a family name – the colonial administration even cheated them of that. No trace of them is left.

The return to their country has come as a shock. Freedom has cost them dear.

LAV'STORY
14 RUE LETORT, PARIS (75018)
FRANCE, 2019

Imane enjoys hanging out at the laundrette on the corner of her street. It's practically empty most of the time and she can daydream in peace, with only damp laundry for company.

She appreciates its name: Lav'Story. Although the sixty-something Chinese proprietor, a man whose eyebrows are fixed in a permanent frown, appears in no mood for a *love story*. No, he looks unhappy and preoccupied, his eyes crammed with worries, his mouth muttering as he cleans the portholes of the tumble dryers. A black cloud hovers above that tiny head of his supported by his fevered neck.

Imane finds it hard to imagine a man like him enjoying romantic films.

She and her big sister Malika must have replayed the video of *Love Story* a hundred times as teenagers. She kept it secret, but Imane was madly in love with the hero, Oliver Barrett, the rich, white Harvard undergrad ice hockey player. She knew she would never come across anyone like him in Aubervilliers.

Oliver Barrett wasn't the kind of man Yamina and Brahim had in mind to sit on the hard Moroccan-style sofa – or sedari – in their living room.

Oliver Barett wasn't the kind of man they had in mind for Imane, period.

Whenever she meets a boy, Imane carries out a little experiment: she pictures him sitting on one of the sofa benches in her mother's living room. She calls this 'the sedari test' and the results are striking, with, at present, a failure rate of 99.9 per cent. No boy belongs there.

What on earth would an Oliver Barrett do on the Taleb family sedari? What of interest could he possibly have to say to Yamina? How could he even hope to impress Brahim?

The sedari test is ruthless.

COMMUNE OF ARBOUZE
PROVINCE OF MSIRDA FOUAGA
ALGERIA, 1964

It proves to be Yamina's single act of disobedience. Until this point, the shy and biddable daughter has never caused her parents any worries. Having been a child of war and exile, she now endures poverty, hunger and unprovoked hidings.

At fifteen, she is used to swallowing the bitter aftertaste of revolution without complaining.

Yamina has barely recovered from the cholera outbreak among the village families a few weeks earlier. She looks like a forlorn skeleton. All you notice are the vast honey-coloured eyes that still light up her furrowed face.

On this day, the woman they call the *old mother* is doing the rounds of the villages in the commune, to tattoo the young girls. Rahma has worn a tattoo on her brow and chin since she was thirteen, and it's time for her daughter to be marked in turn. This tribal legacy has been passed down through the female line for centuries, from generation to generation, and symbolises membership of the tribe. In the Berber tradition, tattooing also marks a rite of passage, from childhood to adulthood.

But wasn't Yamina born directly into adulthood? Didn't the war deprive her of being a child? Has she not already been marked?

Her mother has asked her to prepare the bread for the tattoo woman. Resigned to her fate, Yamina drags her skinny frame out to the yard, readying herself for what lies ahead. She pictures the old mother nicking her skin by drawing a motif, probably the same as Rahma's: a line between the eyebrows with tiny diagonal markings on either side, representing the palm leaf, which embodies *the mother protectress*.

She mustn't move, of course, or cry out, or even whimper. She must be strong. Same as always.

Yamina will feel the warm blood running over her eyebrows before it trickles down her perfect nose. She imagines the tattooist rubbing her charcoal-coated fingers into the gashes, and already she can sense her face flaring up.

According to the women's tales, you are changed afterwards, you belong to your people's history, and, above all, you are protected. They say the custom has a magical purpose: *when the blood has run, the bad luck is over.*

In her heart, Yamina doesn't believe in this nonsense.

If it were so, then why hadn't all these tattooed faces, all these patterns, all these motifs on the women's scratched countenances prevented their bad luck?

You might think the opposite was the case. You might say it was because of their superstitions that they attracted bad luck.

The scorching heat makes her head spin and this time, instead of fetching the semolina from the cloth sack as planned, instead of kneading the dough, instead of lighting the wood in the clay oven, Yamina, in a flash of madness, leaves the mechta by the back door and takes flight.

She shrugs off her apron, raises up the hem of her dress and runs full pelt down the slopes, without once looking back. She won't accept the tattoo, she refuses to be marked for life, she has made up her mind, this tradition will stop at her.

Yamina wishes to keep her face intact, just as God made it.

For the first time in her life, she is deliberately disobeying orders. She understands that spurning this custom will cost her dearly, but she still she runs.

Flat out, rushing over rocky craters, covering perhaps ten kilometres towards the south before she is pulled up short by her body: skin and bone, devoid of strength, no longer her ally.

Yamina's legs are trembling, she can barely stand up. So she crouches, breathless, and weeps, there, on the dry ground, releasing a long sob that has been held prisoner in her throat for months, perhaps for years.

She knows her mother's fury will come crashing down on her head, and her father, returning from the stables where he cleans the horses' hooves all day long for a few coins, will punish her for this affront, for the shame she will have brought upon their household and the whole family, in choosing to run away.

She is afraid.

Yamina wipes away her spittle using the back of her gandoura and scrabbles to her feet. 'We've been through worse than this,' she mutters, using the word with which she urges herself to carry on: 'Nodhi!'

She catches her breath and begins to walk slowly, gazing at the sun nearing its zenith.

The old mother has probably gone on her way by now. Yamina braces herself for her punishment, which she will need to brave with her head held high. She recalls her heroine, Djamila Bouhired. How she laughed in the face of the military tribunal of the French colonial regime when her death sentence was announced. Rebellious laughter in the face of injustice.

If only Yamina had sprung from the womb of this woman; if Djamila had been *her* mother, then she wouldn't have had to flee. Djamila cherished freedom too highly; she would never have inflicted this on her daughter, never have forced her to get her forehead tattooed.

Yamina's forehead belongs to her alone, it represents her *personal liberation front*, her struggle, the first one.

And she will win, even if it means receiving a thrashing and wetting herself under her father's blows.

Yamina's *forehead will be free*: her personal liberation front will remain intact until the grave.

CHEMIN DES VIGNES, COMMUNE OF BOBIGNY DEPARTMENT OF SEINE-SAINT-DENIS (93300) FRANCE, 2019

It's been a long night.

Omar has neckache and can't check the wing mirrors without wincing.

This evening, he picked up a passenger at Montparnasse station and dropped her off at Romainville. He wished the trip could have lasted until dawn. You could even say they got to know one another a little, since they didn't just chat about the weather, or the traffic, or the Gilets Jaunes protests. No, it was more than that.

Omar hopes she hasn't noticed his bald patch, because he didn't have time to shave his head. Unfortunately, when his hair starts growing back, it does so anarchically, tracing a pattern as uneven as the creeks around l'île du Frioul in Marseille. Omar spent his holidays there last year, with the Barcelona FC beach towel he bought back in the bled in 2012, at Tlemcen. The vendor was also called Omar, as he recalls, a friendly guy, skinny, shamelessly exhibiting a thatch of chest curls through his open shirt.

The passenger introduced herself spontaneously, which was handy, because Omar was intimidated, and felt it would have been overstepping the mark to ask for her name...

Nadia, that's what she's called. Her eyes, with their heavy lids, are so black you can barely see the contour of her pupils. She has perfect eyebrows, rounded cheeks and nothing that escapes her lips is surplus, not a word out of place. Omar feels a warm tingling in his chest every time she laughs. This has never happened before. He's never found a girl so special.

Despite her outgoing nature, it's unusual for Nadia to engage taxi drivers in conversation. They tend to be interested in the sound of their own voices, relying on ready-made expressions pinched from Radio Monte Carlo talk shows.

What's attractive about this guy is he doesn't realise it.

Nadia instantly finds his shyness touching, as she does his habit of lowering his head and scrunching his eyes when he smiles. She is moved by his voice, not to mention his forearms and hands, which is all she can see from the back seat.

He's ten times better IRL than in his photo, she reckons, glancing at his driver profile. *He's no fool, he looks cultured and intelligent.*

'So how come you're a taxi driver?' Nadia asks Omar – whose name she's read on the app – sensing his rightful place isn't behind the steering wheel.

'I'm just doing this short term.'

He puts on his hazard lights when they reach rue Gabriel Husson, where the thoroughfare narrows due to the roadworks. The cranes rise up like limbless monsters over Romainville. Omar helps Nadia get her suitcase out of the boot, wishing her a pleasant evening and all the best. He hesitates briefly, conscious of his heart pounding in his chest, and then with no idea how he plucks up the courage. It's a rare event, given that Omar isn't courageous by nature.

'Maybe I'm out of line,' he says, looking into Nadia's dark eyes, 'but I'd like us to stay in touch.'

She smiles. 'Fine,' she says, as if it were the easiest thing in the world.

She gives him her Facebook name and they part.

Omar's going to have to get his arse into gear and create a Facebook profile. He hasn't needed one before this evening.

He thinks about Nadia before he drifts off to sleep and the following morning, too, on waking. Before long, he's wondering whether she was just being polite: why would a girl like her be interested in a boy like him? Omar's old complexes rise to the surface, like a corpse chucked into the water by an assassin in a rush. *She probably didn't dare say no,* they'd spent a nice moment together and she didn't want to embarrass him afterwards. *She's a well brought up girl.*

Pity, Maman would've liked her, he can't help reflecting, much as it bugs him to be thinking this way so early on.

And Omar is on the nose, Nadia is just the kind of girl to win Yamina's approval, despite the fact that she isn't blonde, her skin isn't very white and she doesn't have blue eyes.

As a romantically inclined boy hampered by an excess of shyness, Omar has always struggled to find his way in the world.

His speciality is to be the *best friend.* The confidant who can be counted on, and who becomes desexualised in the process.

It's always been like this, at least since the lycée where he would fall in love with a girl, too fast, often for no obvious reason. All it took was for her to be nice to him, to smile or look him in the eye and that was it, bam. Omar Taleb had a stunning talent for falling in love.

He maintained the friendship in the hope that it would head in a new direction, over time, but the new direction turned out to be full-on fiasco.

The girl ended up seeking his advice about how she should approach *another boy,* who was frequently more attractive, more butch or more mysterious. Long story short, he was bound to possess some attribute Omar lacked.

The girl invariably fell for a jerk who was into her body, which hadn't even fully matured, and which he, the jerk, could as easily trade for another body. The kind of guy who didn't care about her, or her feelings. No, it was all about the body, end of, the same body Omar hardly dared glance at, because by the age of seventeen he possessed an overdeveloped sense of prudishness, and, nice boy that he was, Omar listened to the girl and encouraged her, without revealing his own feelings. He didn't want to hurt her, so he didn't tell her which way it was heading, even though it was clear it was going to the wall. Oh yes, he knew this story's ending off by heart. And he was never wrong. Once the boy had cheated on her, given her a rough ride and jilted her, the girl was back to cry on Omar's reassuring chest *as a friend* and, nice boy that he was, he consoled her without trying to take advantage of the situation. He knew the right words. It has always been his job to mend broken hearts, so much so he's forgotten about his own, heart that is. When the girl says: 'You're so kind, Omar, you're a true friend,' Omar makes do.

He's out of sync.

An Arab who doesn't conform to the world's expectations of him: as in, becoming a dominant, physical, butch, conquering, testosterone-fuelled man who is also untrustworthy, and even, where possible, dangerous.

Omar will need to invent his own way of being a man.

From what he's observed, real men never say 'I love you'. For them, doing so would constitute an appalling sign of weakness.

In the westerns his father watches on television, there's a flickering stream of humdrum images. The moment always comes when the cowboy grabs a woman, any woman, takes her by the arm and grips her tightly. As he pulls himself up to his full height and stares straight into her eyes, he decides to press her roughly against him. His actions are virile, borderline bestial, and he grunts and growls, like someone raised by wolves, or the riot police.

Occasionally, the woman puts up a fight, panting and softly urging: 'Johnny nooo, please, nooo.' But her whispers are scarcely audible, and Johnny doesn't give a damn, since Johnny, like all cowboys, mistakes no for yes.

It's clear she's not having a great time of it upstairs in this New Mexico saloon. How many days has it been, she wonders, while trying to free herself from the cowboy's grip, since he last hosed himself down? For the cowboy stinks. And while we're on the subject, does anyone know why cowboys shower fully clothed? They bathe in a sort of revolting cotton onesie for grown-ups, a quick dip in a wooden barrel set up in the middle of the living room, no soap, no massage glove, no shower gel and, I repeat, FULLY CLOTHED.

How did these people carry out a genocide against millions of Indigenous Americans and invent Hollywood?

As for the woman, all that wriggling and writhing to escape Johnny's muscular arms messes up her hair, which eventually flops over her face, making her even more beautiful in the cowboy's eyes.

Nobody's broached the issue of consent, that much is clear. She looks unwilling from the off, and, if her body language is anything to go by, she's keen to break free, but as for our cowboy, he couldn't care less about whether she consents or not. He shakes her up some more, then entices her with his lips. It's worth pointing out here he hasn't got any lips to speak of, he's Mister White Cowboy No Lips, but with a hat to die for. Oh and he's a rubbish kisser, anyone can see that.

The girl stops putting up a fight. Just as we're wondering how things are going to pan out, CUT. We jump to a black screen, no fade, and it's... the following morning, in a bedroom offering rudimentary levels of comfort, a crucifix hanging on the wall, a chamber pot and a tune on a harmonica. The girl is in the background, out of focus, lying with her back to us, under the sheet.

That's all, folks.

No more information, we can't even tell if she's dead or alive. As for the cowboy, he pulls on his boots while smoking a roll-up and exits without looking back. No *salam*, no *thank you*, no siree.

Clearly, in the butch stakes, Omar has some catching up to do.

At Porsay beach, a few years ago, his cousin Youcef came over all serious on his case, sunning himself on a Barcelona FC towel while Omar, the towel's rightful owner, got his thighs scorched on the hot sand. Youcef decided to give his cousin one hell of a lesson in the art of seduction.

That summer, he instructed Omar to chat up the badly dressed girls, or else the fat ones. 'Get your hand in, they're the best. You've got a one hundred per cent chance of them saying yes if you ask them out, plus they'll give you ratings for choosing them, you get me, they'll be faithful and in love. You can do what you like with them.'

Not only did Omar find it kind of crude when Youcef pointed out the girls, to illustrate his B.B. theory (Bled Bozo was Hannah's nickname for their cousin); but, unfortunately for Omar, the approach didn't pay off either. Going out with girls he didn't have the hots for wasn't the worst of it. No, to add insult to injury they were the ones giving *him* a hard time.

Being humiliated by uglies wasn't great for his self-esteem.

And to think, back then, Omar still had hair.

COMMUNE OF AÏN KIHAL
WILAYA OF AÏN TÉMOUCHENT
ALGERIA, 1967

At eighteen, Yamina is an exceptionally pretty young woman who turns heads without realising it.

She doesn't check herself in the mirror, or understand the effect of her honey gaze, communicating as it does both strength and sadness. She isn't aware of how her delicate gestures make hearts skip a beat, or the thick lustrousness of her eyelashes, or the radiance of her cheeks, or the beauty of her brown curly locks, forever tangled in her green headscarf.

There is no mirror, and, even if there were one, she would be too busy to dwell on her own reflection.

Yamina is an unacknowledged beauty.

Ten families live at the old farm, in the heart of the countryside of Aïn Kihal. The fathers, all former combatants, came into several hectares a few years after Independence (as is the case for those who've provided proof of their role in the War of Liberation).

God knows the most deserving aren't necessarily the best

rewarded. But that's another story...

These mujahideen-turned-farmers-again divide up the labour and harvests between them. They do their best to lift their families out of poverty, in cheery communist spirit. Mohamed Madouri is proud to display his card attesting to his status as a former combatant, even if he is incapable of reading what's written on it.

For all that Yamina's father may be illiterate, he is a gifted orator chosen by the other comrades to represent them at the regional farmers' union.

Life is less harsh from now on, and the Madouri family is no longer hungry.

From first cockerel's crow to final evening prayer, life on the farm is a flurry of activity. In the mornings, Yamina must feed the animals, do the housework, get her younger brothers and sisters ready for school and accompany them as far as the tractor that belongs to generous Monsieur Teyeb.

He owns one of those monstrous orange Massey Fergusons, and all the kids from the old farm pile into its rusty trailer for the five-kilometre journey separating them from the town.

Monsieur Teyeb never had any children of his own, but he does the school run for every child.

Each morning, whatever the weather, he rises at dawn, prays, drinks his tea, pulls on his rubber boots, starts up his engine and helps the kids climb up, one by one. Some are still reeling with sleepiness, having scarcely had time to spit-wash their eyes.

When it's bitterly cold, kind Monsieur Teyeb covers the trailer with a layer of straw. It's not so different from looking after his sheep, and all about making do with what's to hand.

The smaller children sit or crouch, huddled against or on top of one another to stay warm. The canny ones, first in, lean their elbows against the sacks of wheat piled at the back, since this journey doubles as a mill run on behalf of the farmers.

On the road, he makes them practise patriotic songs lest these kids forget their fathers' struggles. And in winter, singing 'Min Djibalina' – From Our Mountains – helps them warm up their poor stiff bodies.

From our mountains the singing of free men rang out,
    calling us to Independence,
Calling us to Independence, the Independence of our
    nation.
Our sacrifice for the nation is more important than life.
I sacrifice my life and my property for you.
O my country, O my country, I only love you.
My heart has forgotten the world, it is lost in your love.
Everything grows in the rich earth of your love.

May there come a day when life is joyous!
We defend every spoor on your soil with our souls:
We are the sons of lions, so let us face your enemies.
Your rank in History shines down on your uplands.
Your imposing landscapes acclaim your beauty.
We are your enclosing wall, your steady mountains:
We are the sons of Algeria,
a resolute and resilient people.

They cling on with all their might to avoid going over the side of the trailer and crash-landing in the cactuses by the roadside. If you can call it a road, when it's more of a muddy unnavigable track.

Perhaps a few of these children, the pluckiest, those brave enough not to abandon their studies, will rise above their condition of being farmers' sons. Who knows? Monsieur Teyeb maintains a cast-iron belief that it will be so. It is this hope that prompts him to start up his tractor every morning.

Monsieur Teyeb likes to imagine there's a future pilot on board his beloved Massey Ferguson. To pilot an aeroplane, now that *would* be something. Piercing the sky is of a different order to zigzagging the fields in a tractor. When he sees an airliner passing through the clouds above his head, Monsieur Teyeb stands still, briefly, in the middle of his plot, and daydreams beneath this ironmongery bird before returning to his task.

The Massey Ferguson and the kind-hearted farmer

who drove it enabled those children to study, to become teachers and insurance agents. Others gave up and joined their fathers back in the fields. But Monsieur Teyeb lives on in their collective memory, together with his old woollen hat covered in fluff and the patriotic songs belted out in the early morning mist.

Yamina spends the rest of her day sewing. This is how she fills her 'free' time, ever since her father rescued an old Singer sewing machine, dating from the start of the century, found on a property deserted by a Pied-Noir family. Mohamed Madouri brought back this plunder from the European settlers, in the hope that his daughter might do something with it.

Yamina makes dresses and underskirts for the women. She has also learned how to knit, using improvised needles: poultry feathers to start with, then, later on, two iron spokes from an old bicycle wheel at the dump. She is talented and meticulous, spending hours at the machine, her foot on the pedal, eyes narrowed, focused on her handiwork.

Thanks to her output, by the end of the wedding season she has managed to set aside hundreds of dinars, which is no small achievement, but she can't stop thinking about Monsieur Teyeb driving her brothers towards a more promising future in his Massey Ferguson. What wouldn't she give to huddle in that tractor, even if it meant bending over backwards, even if it meant being transported like a goat? What wouldn't Yamina give for the opportunity to attend school again, to sit in a classroom for one more day, to hear the scrape of chalk against blackboard, to recite poetry in her favourite lesson? What wouldn't she give to write with a pen again and for her head to spin from sniffing the inkwell?

One day, she resolved to part with the schoolgirl's apron she had secretly kept for years at the back of the sideboard. She cut it up to make dusters.

COMMUNE OF AUBERVILLIERS
DEPARTMENT OF SEINE-SAINT-DENIS (93300)
FRANCE, 2019

Yamina admires all of God's creatures, but it bothers her when the neighbour's diabetic mutt, who is half-blind, rubs itself against her in the lift. She never dares say so and has to devise all sorts of dog-avoidance tactics.

It drives Hannah nuts. 'Why are the French always trying to make us love their hounds? As if being a dog lover made you a better patriot. Liking dogs proves nothing. Not liking them doesn't prove anything either.'

Yamina knows that some owners sleep with their dogs on the bed, they let them lick their faces, they get their names engraved on their collars, buy them coats with pompoms and walk them in all weathers, at all hours of the day or night. Yamina doesn't always understand this, but she accepts *it's their way of life*. She finds them more devoted to their hounds than they are to their own family.

If they'd prefer to take care of their dogs while their senile parents roam the corridors of some nursing home in baggy pyjamas, so be it.

Yamina would like to avoid physical contact with dogs, end of story. No need to make a fuss about it. It would be out of character for Yamina to make a fuss.

She had plenty of dogs for company in Algeria, which was hardly surprising, given that she was a farmer's daughter. Her dogs were all called Bobby, every one of them, without exception. All dogs are called Bobby in Algeria, and none of them complains about identity complexes. Bobbies have no problem determining who's who among themselves, they don't hold their name against their owners, they don't have a favourite brand of dogfood, and they don't suffer from gluten intolerance either. Also, *son of a dog* is a common insult deployed throughout the country, and no canine lobby has ever brought a case on those grounds.

In Algeria, a dog knows exactly what to do: round up the stray sheep and return them to the flock.

In Yamina's eyes, ending up in a two-bed apartment, in a social housing block, with communal heating and grotty lino, is not an acceptable fate for a dog. At least her Bobbies could run free across the plains and defecate where they saw fit, without having to jump up and down, barking for their owners to get out of bed and take them for a pee.

If she wants to avoid the neighbour's dog sniffing her rear, Yamina is obliged to take a step backwards on the landing.

The neighbour's reaction is always the same: 'He won't eat you, don't be frightened. Isn't that right, Kaiser, you're a nice boy, aren't you? Who's a nice doggie, eh? Mummy's nice little doggie…' The neighbour can barely disguise her sadistic laugh and almost lets the dog have his way, neglecting to shorten his lead. 'He won't bite you, he won't hurt you, you mustn't be frightened of him,' she says, stroking her bow-wow and spreading his obnoxious smell, which makes Yamina gag. She holds her breath, discreetly. The neighbour reckons her English beagle scares Yamina. She assumes knowledge of her fears. If she could only imagine everything this woman has had to contend with. *The truth is, it's Kaiser who should be afraid of Yamina and take a step backwards when she passes by.*

Yamina gives a friendly smile while shaking the bottom of her djellaba, then looks at the dog and thinks back to how she treated her first Bobby. She wants to say to Kaiser: 'You have no idea how lucky you are!'

Yamina avoids Kaiser for the simple reason that she prays, and, in order to pray, you must be in a state of purity, having performed wudu, the ritual washing. Coming into contact with a dog invalidates that state of purity, so you have to start the ritual washing again. Yamina would like to explain this to her neighbour. It's not complicated. After all, Yamina wears the hijab, she is Muslim and she makes no secret of this fact.

Contrary to what people say, there's nothing suspicious about this, nothing shifty. She could perfectly well explain to her neighbour that no, she's doesn't have the heebie-jeebies about being bitten, she has nothing personal against

Kaiser, she could just say: 'I would like to remain in a state fit for prayer, so I am politely asking you to respect my beliefs and to keep a hold on your dog's lead when I go past.' It need only happen just the once, a single explanation given with mutual respect, and then this scene, as embarrassing for Yamina and the neighbour as it is for the dog, would never be repeated.

Or Yamina could simply *not want* the dog to approach her, without any other justification. That's her prerogative.

It could be so straightforward.

But something prevents Yamina from having the conversation with this woman who has lived in the same building for at least ten years. The same woman Yamina holds the door open for: '*Bonjour, comment ça va, madame?*' To whom she's always pleasant, to whose home she sends Omar with a plate of msemen (square Moroccan waxy pancakes) or baghrir (Algerian spongy pancakes with thousands of tiny holes). Yamina loves sharing her cooking with her neighbours.

They indulge and return the plates empty, sometimes weeks later, sometimes not at all. To return an empty plate is, for Yamina, shameful, for it demonstrates a basic lack of understanding. The Taleb family is generous, they enjoy sharing and, as in so many families, this custom is handed down from generation to generation: *always return the plates with a little something on them*. The neighbours don't understand this, and Yamina doesn't hold it against them. But, as a result, her dinner services are incomplete and she regularly has to acquire more plates from Nina Bazar, the Moroccan shop on the Nationale 2, between Quatre-Chemins and Fort d'Aubervilliers, over by the Jewish cemetery. It's a temple to crockery, where you'll also find spices, curtains, rosaries, white musk, lampshades, shampoo and boxes of Ariel.

Yamina, who is by nature optimistic, who refuses to see the bad in anything, can sense, to her dismay, that the atmosphere is changing. These are different times from the eighties, when she was in her mid-thirties, her children were small, and the primary school teachers used to ask politely if she wouldn't mind translating for the other mothers. Perhaps, back then, things were simply less in-your-face. Yamina tends to embellish her memories.

Yamina feels that, today, we can no longer really say *who we are*.

Who we are has become too risky.

She worries for her children and for all children like them. She asks Omar to switch off the television when he has the news channel on continuously. It makes her feel queasy.

As a matter of principle, she refuses to utter the names of the columnists or Islamophobe polemicists granted airspace to slobber their hatred. She would rather dub them Woujah el-kelb (Dog Face), Aawouj el-foum (Twisted Mouth), or Seum al-aalam (World's Venom).

It makes her children laugh when she calls them by these nicknames. They can't get enough of it, and it helps to de-escalate the situation, to the point where they almost forget the violence behind the words they've just heard. Yamina remains calm about such attempts to rob her kids of legitimacy: 'I don't know why you get so hot and bothered. What do I care, even if they want to rip off my headscarf, they'll never rip out my heart, more's the pity for them, because that's where my faith is!'

Chances are the neighbour also listens to the rantings of Dog Face, Twisted Mouth and World's Venom.

And Hannah, who lacks Yamina's patience, doesn't hold back, telling their neighbour drily: 'Keep a hold of your dog, please, I don't want him coming near me.'

Later, she complains to her sisters. 'They do my head in. Since we've been here, we've done the work of learning how to live with them, so why is it always on us to make the effort? Enough already, it's on everyone! I'm not here to make them feel better about themselves, and if they're too stupid to figure out we're also human beings, that's not my problem. Them and us, I'm telling you, it's like an organ transplant that won't take.'

'That's just the way it is, binti, and we have to accept it,' Yamina says, thinking she can placate her daughter. 'It's like we're their guests, and we're visiting their home.'

Which only fires Hannah up even more.

'No, we're not in their home, Maman! And we're not "guests"! Did you ever receive an invite? Because I didn't! I've had enough, I've been listening to this rubbish for thirty-five years. This is our home. We were born here! And our coming here was hardly a coincidence!'

At the rate things are going, it's not difficult for Hannah to picture the day when her 'Arab' is the person she'll have to keep on a tight lead, and, if he doesn't stand well back, someone will feel compelled to say: 'He won't eat you, don't be frightened. Isn't that right, Karim, you're a nice Arab boy, aren't you? Who's a nice Arab, eh? Mummy's nice little Arab...'

Yamina is forever begging her not to make a scene and, despite her big gob, Hannah is an obedient daughter. Otherwise, she'd long ago have given the neighbour's dog one almighty kick.

Each generation must, out of relative obscurity, discover its mission, fulfil it, or betray it.

Frantz Fanon, *The Wretched of the Earth*

COMMUNE OF AÏN KIHAL
WILAYA OF AÏN TÉMOUCHENT
ALGERIA, 1978

Yamina felt as if Algeria had lost a father.

It was the month of December, and she was finishing off an order of a dozen turtleneck sweaters, plus long socks, to be sent to immigrant worker cousins in Grenoble. Everybody knew the winters came harsher in France. Yamina found her thoughts turning to these men when she had to defrost the freezer. She who had never seen snow.

'No other president,' Mohamed Madouri liked to remind his family, 'will ever achieve the stature of Boumediene.' But was he really a good and righteous man? A patriot who wanted to build a future for his freshly liberated country? No one in the family ever asked such questions: Boumediene had arrived as a saviour, and that put a stop to any challenges.

So, Yamina took her father's and brothers' word for it, admiring this man with his fierce expression. She was unaware of the fratricidal war that had taken place, and far from imagining that Algeria would live under a fratricidal sky for a long time to come.

COMMUNE OF AUBERVILLIERS
DEPARTMENT OF SEINE–SAINT–DENIS (93300)
FRANCE, 2019

Malika is the eldest of the siblings, and yet she is the one you notice least, the one who never makes waves. At parents' evenings, teachers would say: 'Ah, if all our students were like Malika, the classroom would be paradise.' Her nose was constantly buried in a book. And, for a long time, she believed in a meritocracy.

She only leaves the house to go to work, attend a talk or event, or take in an exhibition. She occupies the least space in the family wardrobe, purchased in 1994 in ten interest-free instalments, because she sees no point in owning many clothes. Not that finding clothes is easy when you're a size XL–XXL. She doesn't do superficial, either, refusing to dye her hair, despite Imane's best efforts to persuade her otherwise. Malika is fast approaching forty and a fine crop of white hairs. In truth, she likes this proof that she is her mother's daughter.

On Saturday afternoons at home, in front of an American soap on Télé Monte Carlo, she sometimes does

Yamina's hair, while reckless teenagers with no helmets rev mopeds outside, doing wheelies, making a diabolical din. Malika sighs: 'Don't come crying when there's a serious accident!' Yamina shakes her head. 'It's just one more way of making their mothers suffer! May God preserve them, they don't realise.' Malika is less forgiving: 'What d'you mean they don't realise? Afterwards, there'll be a fundraising page on Leetchi.com and messages like *RIP Mamadou, a brother departed too soon*.' Yamina often wonders why the children of poor parents behave so dangerously.

Malika relishes these moments with her mother, to whom she dedicates plenty of her free time. Since securing her civil service job at Bobigny registry office, she's the new pride of her family, generating almost as much buzz as Omar. Almost.

Malika conditions her mother's hair with the organic avocado oil she buys at the discount pharmacy in Quatre-Chemins, which makes it go all shiny, enhancing Yamina's magnificent shades of natural grey. She has a thick white tuft at the front, giving her the appearance of a saint wearing a cloud.

Her mother has never been more beautiful, Malika reflects, gently combing Yamina's hair and coaxing it into a long plait that reaches the middle of her back. She approves of her mother still wearing her hair long as she approaches seventy.

Why do white women suddenly decide to cut their hair short when they turn fifty? You'd think it was mandatory. Malika wonders if there isn't a special organisation tasked with sending out an official letter after their fiftieth birthday, like one of those reminders to make your mammogram appointment. Perhaps they already know, they're expecting it, just like their mother and grandmother before them.

> *Dear Nadine,*
> *Now that you're fifty, it's time to book in for your pixie haircut at a salon of your choice, preferably a branch of Jean Louis David or Fabio Salsa conveniently located in your nearest shopping centre.*
> *NB: You can always ask for extra hairspray.*

During this rite of passage, a pair of glasses with fancy purple arms, to match the haircut, is often added to the mix.

One day, towards the end of the noughties, Yamina suddenly stopped buying hair dye at the supermarket. It was ridiculous, a never-ending faff that took up an insane amount of her time: barely two weeks after she'd applied the dye, a white line would appear. She used to buy l'Oréal's Excellence Crème in Dark Copper Mahogany after seeing it on Andie MacDowell in a TV advert.

Plus, it felt too much like hard work. She had to wear her reading glasses, the ones from the pharmacy that were too big for her petite face, with plastic arms that didn't grip. But without them it was impossible to read the instructions-in-five-easy-steps. Despite using the same brand umpteen times, Yamina still liked to read the instructions.

So, one day, Yamina decided to break with this ritual. It wasn't as if she was dyeing her hair to look nice for Brahim: she could have the same hairdo as Bozo the Clown and he would still think she was beautiful.

She simply let her white hair grow. It took years, and if Andie MacDowell did the same, heaps of other women would probably quit dyeing too, perhaps they'd feel less alone, and they would grow old together, in sisterhood, without bitterness or ammonia.

COMMUNE OF AÏN KIHAL
WILAYA OF AÏN TÉMOUCHENT
ALGERIA, 1981

Yamina could see only his hands.

As he signed the marriage certificate for the civil ceremony at the Mairie de la Daïra, she discreetly raised her gaze, and – through her white hayek, wrapped around her for modesty, protecting her from the world – she stared at his enormous hands.

She had never seen such hands.

Had she just married a giant? An ogre?

Brahim Taleb's signature was wobbly, his fingers dwarfing the pen lent by the qadi, or Muslim judge. Even the pneumatic drills he gripped on building sites across France looked like children's toys in his hands.

For the occasion, Yamina was accompanied by her brother Moussa and her sister-in-law Soumaya. The couple had met at the École Mohamed-Harchaoui in Aïn Témouchent, where both were teachers, and had married the previous summer in a love match. Yamina embroidered their bed linen, prepared the sheepskins and crocheted their blankets, without much in the way of thanks from her brother.

Before arriving at the Mairie de la Daïra, Moussa, who drove a black Renault 16 at the time, stopped in the town centre, on the main boulevard of Aïn Témouchent. At his suggestion, the three of them paid a visit to Berrichi, the commune's photographer, to have their portrait taken. Chez Berrichi featured a giant poster on the back wall with a backdrop of a beach and palm trees, as was popular in photography studios across Algeria.

Yamina didn't smile in the photograph. She didn't want to go to France, viewing her departure for Paris much as a condemned person might contemplate their execution date. Today was meant to be a celebration, but Moussa understood that his big sister was in no party mood.

At the Mairie, Yamina trembled with shyness. She felt a sense of shame at marrying past thirty, when all the girls of her generation had been gone since the age of fifteen or sixteen, promptly producing babies. Country girls marry young, especially those on the farms.

Yamina had become the local spinster, the one everyone would mock, which was why she had agreed, reluctantly, to marry this immigrant ten years her senior: Brahim Taleb.

The years came and went, as did the suitors, or at least they did at the beginning, until Mohamed Madouri had systematically rejected all the men who had asked for

Yamina's hand in marriage. Not that he was particularly fussy, but, he still needed his eldest daughter who, in his own words, *was worth more than all his six sons put together.*

He couldn't manage without her help on the farm. This was in addition to everything she did in the house, where she was responsible for her brothers' and sisters' education, as well as contributing to the household expenses by dint of her sewing and even taking care of the beehive, which produced delicious honey. More than a biddable daughter, she was his right arm. But after Yamina's twenty-fifth birthday, no more suitors presented themselves to Mohamed Madouri.

The only person who wanted Yamina was this man of forty-something, who had spent his life down mines and on construction sites, experiencing nothing but exile and working men's hostels. Aïcha, the sister of Brahim Taleb, lived at the old farm with her husband, and it was she who suggested her brother marry Yamina. She admired the Madouri family and thought their daughter would be perfect for him: courageous and hard-working.

The arrangement was struck one afternoon, after Friday prayers. On returning to the house, Mohamed Madouri summoned his wife and asked her to speak with Yamina.

Rahma did not greet this news with joy but obeyed her husband, as was her custom.

The last word was left to their daughter, but did she really have a choice? Her assent was more of a formality.

For nights on end, Yamina sobbed into the privacy of her pillow, whose slip had been crocheted by her own hands.

After jealously keeping her close to him, how had her father resolved to send her across the Mediterranean, to live in the country of those colonisers he had driven with such fervour out of his own?

AUBERVILLIERS ALLOTMENTS
DEPARTMENT OF SEINE-SAINT-DENIS (93300)
FRANCE, 2019

Two paces from Route Nationale 2, five minutes on foot from Fort d'Aubervilliers métro station, Line 7, close to Zingaro's renowned equestrian circus, and not far from the roar of the giant intersection between Pantin, Aubervilliers and la Courneuve, lies Yamina's little paradise.

A plot of land measuring about a hundred and fifty square metres, an allotment that the community gardens association of Aubervilliers assigned to the Taleb family in May 2007.

Escorting Yamina to her plot for the first time, Marie-Claire, the association's representative, told her, thinking little of it: 'You're very lucky, there's a magnificent fig tree on this one!'

Every year, the tree provides Yamina with delicious figs at the summer's end. She harvests bowlfuls of them, and no matter how many she gives to her friends or neighbours, the figs keep growing. It's as if the more she gives, the more this tree provides. And then come the jams.

She thinks back to the fig tree of her childhood, the one

that perished at Msirda. From now on, Yamina's tree, her baraka, her good fortune, is no longer to be found in Algeria, but here, in Aubervilliers, strong-rooted and generous.

Bet she'll plant rows and rows of mint, then potatoes an' broad beans, then more potatoes... This is what Manuel, who gardened the adjoining plot, had reckoned when his new neighbour arrived twelve years earlier. *Ai, las patatas, eh? Only thing those Arabs know how to plant.*

Brahim felt obliged to dust off his rudimentary Portuguese for the benefit of Manuel, who eventually admitted, with some embarrassment: 'I'm Spanish, M'sieur.'

Since his retirement from the construction sites, Brahim hadn't had much occasion to practise his Portuguese, except when it came to insulting other drivers who lacked basic road etiquette, at which point he'd test drive all the expletives he knew: '*Porra, sacana, cabrão.*'

Sometimes, he'd mash up his Mediterranean outbursts, resulting in: '*Vai te foder Ya l'Hmar!*'. In other words shouting 'Go fuck yourself' in Portuguese, while calling the person a 'donkey' in Arabic.

In no time, it became *Yamina's garden*. Brahim was responsible for weeding and barbecues. Yamina took care of the rest, and, contrary to Spanish Manuel's expectations, she didn't plant broad beans or potatoes. She began with flowers, French marigolds.

Yamina forgets everything while gardening, and sometimes

she even sings, only stopping to make her prayers in the shed.

Before, she used to pray on the cool grass in fine weather. This daughter of the earth enjoyed the sense of connection, the energy from the ground as she prostrated herself, the immensity of the sky above her head. It was pleasant to pray in the open air, that much was sure. But she no longer does so. She doesn't feel safe. Yamina would rather hide these days.

Especially since the case of that mother stabbed for wearing a headscarf.

Yes, *who we are* has become complicated, and Yamina's thoughts gravitate to this with increasing frequency.

When tending her flowers, her rosemary and peas, she wears a white lab coat that used to belong to Hannah back when she studied physics and chemistry at the lycée.

Yamina has a full set of work gear, including the gloves she picked up for €6.99 at Bricorama on avenue Jean Lolive in Pantin, and a pair of nearly new, black Air Maxes, the ones with the pink swoosh. Imane left them behind for her mother when she moved out; there was only so much she could take to her twenty-square-metre studio.

'So, farm girl, d'you miss having your nails clogged with earth?' Brahim sometimes teases her.

Yamina doesn't find this especially funny. 'Your sister's the farm girl,' she replies, and carries on planting shallots, on her knees, while he takes in the Auber sun, stretched out on a plastic deckchair, toes exposed.

The truth is that Brahim envies his wife's talent. For all he was king of the spade, it turns out that digging a métro station and gardening aren't the same thing. Brahim may be a strong man but he's not a patient one, still less a precise one, and both are necessary qualities in a gardener.

You would swear the lines on Yamina's plot were drawn with a ruler, since not a single leaf strays over the mark. Everything is orderly and pleasing to the eye. The garden is fertile and blessed, and this jumps out at you. 'It's so calm here,' Malika says, whenever she accompanies her mother at weekends, 'it puts you in the mood for a nap.' And, without fail, Yamina replies: 'Go into the shed and have your siesta, binti, what's stopping you?'

Malika lies down on a bench in the shed and starts drifting off. She's watched her fair share of YouTube tutorials about deep breathing and how to relax each limb in turn in order to fall asleep quickly. She's earned herself a reputation for it at the Mairie de Bobigny, where she is the champion of power naps, locking the door to her work pod during breaks.

Each time they walk past the Talebs' plot, the other allotment holders exclaim: 'Wow, what a beautiful garden you have, madame,' or they whistle in admiration: 'Pffffiou.' Yamina smiles and thanks them, but as soon as the person has left, she is quick to whisper: 'Tabarak Allah', blessed is God. She wants to avert the evil eye and everything withering. You need to protect yourself, and who better for that than God?

BEL-AIR DISTRICT, CITÉ DU ROND-POINT
WILAYA OF ORAN
ALGERIA, 1981

The traditional celebration took place on 29 July 1981, the same day as the marriage of Prince Charles and Lady Diana.

Less than a month later, Yamina and her husband left Algeria for Paris. Well, Aubervilliers.

Leaning from the window of her makeshift bridal suite, up on the seventeenth floor, no lift, in the building where some of her new husband's family live, she fixes her eyes on the figure of her father one last time.

Yamina feels not just unhappy but physically abandoned.

This will be the last sighting she has of her parents for many months to come. True to form, her mother, Rahma, hasn't shed a tear, and heads off down the boulevard without looking back. As for the patriarch, Mohamed Madouri, he tries to mask his guilt, but Yamina clearly sees him looking up, no question about it, glancing one last time at the balcony.

Yamina tells herself that a bride shouldn't weep on her

wedding day, but she can't stem this flow of tears.

It's not panning out the way it does in the seventies Egyptian films she would sometimes watch in the afternoons if she'd finished all her farm chores. Those films featured men declaiming poems and gazing amorously at women who rattled off *habibis* here and *habibis* there: addressing their male suitors as 'darling' and 'beloved', with love always winning the day.

She recalls the expression of Nabil, the youngest of her brothers, twenty-five years her junior, for whom she was much more than a sister. So grief-stricken was he by their separation, he wept until he collapsed. It was as if Yamina's heart had been ripped out.

Her mother-in-law and sisters-in-law keep inviting her to change dresses and eat something before her husband returns in the evening. Everybody is concerned about her not wanting to leave the bedroom.

Yamina Taleb née Madouri isn't hungry. The young woman wants to take her hair down and remove the make-up which makes her look sad and garish, like a grotesque clown in a travelling circus. She wants to go back to her family and call the whole thing off.

In a few hours, she will be alone with this man, in this bedroom, this man with the huge hands, about whom she knows so little, scarcely more than his name and age. Nobody has told her what she's meant to do, how she should behave in front of him, she doesn't know the drill, hasn't been given any advice.

Her mother wasn't the kind to pass on intimate secrets to her daughter while rubbing her back in the sweaty heat of a hammam.

Yes, becoming a woman is abrupt.

COMMUNE OF AUBERVILLIERS
DEPARTMENT OF SEINE–SAINT–DENIS (93300)
FRANCE, 2019

Omar's bedroom could pass for student accommodation, affording him the illusion of independence at the grand age of twenty-nine. He's been assigned the most spacious room in the apartment. *Happy coincidence?*

A flatscreen measuring one metre seventeen, perched on an Ikea TV unit, Bestå, in walnut-effect light grey, gobbles up the room. It's the only thing you see when you walk in.

Omar bought it from Darty in Porte de la Villette with one of his first pay cheques while working on a short-term contract for Île de France Health Insurance.

He was passed over for a permanent contract in favour of a freshly recruited girl who had caught the eye of their senior line manager. This girl secured the post promised to Omar, even though she lacked the relevant skill set. She was, however, happy to wear short skirts for the benefit of said manager, despite a physique that more closely resembled that of a cockerel than a woman – think big belly, skinny legs.

In his bedroom Omar also has a wardrobe, a Formica coffee

table in imitation pink Tuscan marble, a velvet Moroccan-style banquette which doubles as his bed, and a leatherette office chair where he hunkers down for his PlayStation 4 sessions. He mostly opts for violent games, playing an American GI on the hunt for Arab terrorists.

Omar can game for hours, losing all sense of time as he chats to the other gamers in his broken English, firing instructions through his headset. Scattered across the planet, they're all, like him, locked inside a globalised virtual world, which makes Brahim throw up his hands in despair. 'If I have a heart attack in the room next door, my son won't notice a thing.'

Brahim doesn't understand much about Omar's life. His grown-up-child world dismays him. 'Playing'? At thirty? Chances are, Brahim has never *played*. Except, perhaps, lying on his canvas sack, when he used to imagine the odd shape in the clouds, as a six- or seven-year-old shepherd who led his goats to pasture.

A few childhood memories linger for Brahim, including one particular summer's evening when the region was in the grip of famine. War was raging in Europe, and many of the menfolk had already joined the colonial troops in their efforts to liberate the south of France from German occupation.

Back in the village, Brahim and his brothers were starving, their heads infested with fleas.

Their mother lit a fire in the courtyard and the children

gathered round it, leaning forward to shake their hair and make the fleas jump into the flames, triggering small explosions, like the sound of corn in a pan. Brahim and his brothers hallucinated that night, their hunger fuelling their dreams of a giant popcorn-making ceremony around the fire. *Pop, pop, pop*, in every direction, beneath the starry sky and before the dancing flames, until they could almost smell the fragrant, warm corn.

Brahim, who has an iron constitution, is past eighty now, *may God preserve him*, but the old man is taken aback by this generation of prolonged childhood, reduced responsibilities and limited courage.

Sometimes he tells Yamina that in mollycoddling Omar she has made half a man of him, or so he thinks. He adores his son, but regrets letting his wife overprotect him.

At sixteen, Brahim was down the pit, black-faced, over by Roche la Molière and Firminy, in the Loire region, in the days when coal mining still provided work.

'Yes, but Omar gets up early, he drives all day and sometimes he works nights,' Yamina counters. 'He has back problems and his passengers aren't always easy.' She is mindful of the weakness of her arguments when her husband plays his trump card of the mining company.

Yamina doesn't understand Brahim's determination to toughen up Omar. In her eyes, ensuring their children can enjoy a pleasant, easy life is recompense for the harshness of their own lives, or else what was the point?

Is Omar meant to go down the mine and get his face covered in coal dust to prove to his father that he's a man?

Aren't the Uber drivers of today the miners of yesterday? Aren't they just like their fathers? Aren't these low-paid workers, whose wages yield profits for a greedy and unequal system, their worthy inheritors, after all?

Despite their studies and the opportunities supposedly available to them, these young men drive cars all night long for a pittance, reliant on app alerts that play havoc with their messed-up hearts, reliant on ratings and the comments of a fickle clientele.

Yamina leaves Omar to his never-ending virtual games because she doesn't find this mode of escape excessive. She's grateful to him for never being in police custody, which is no mean feat.

Her only worry is that he will follow in his sisters' footsteps and not marry.

It's while he's cleaning his Renault Talisman (1.5 CC Eco2 Energy Business, leather interior) at Freewash in Aubervilliers, opposite the motorway and close to the wholesale halal butcher, Viande à Gogo, that Omar's thoughts turn to contacting Nadia, his passenger from Romainville. The girl with the smouldering gaze, that makes his heart skip a beat – her charcoal eyes a far cry from the coal down his father's mine.

Every other girl seems bland by comparison. It's as if

there's been magic at work. Nadia has collected the seven crystal balls, just like in his favourite manga, *Dragon Ball*.

Omar finally created his Facebook account. He couldn't find a satisfactory profile photo, so he used a black and white headshot of Zinedine Zidane, his *successful* double. Kind of. An icon. A balding Algerian, like Omar, but with talent. Next, he tried friending his cousins in Algeria, as well as his old classmates, some of whom didn't bother to respond, and for the finishing touch he subscribed to Rafael Nadal's fan page.

Omar's been following tennis tournaments since he was knee-high. Back in the day, he used to dream of becoming a champion, but he was convinced it was a sport for rich kids and never joined a club. 'We don't have the means to pay for a tennis club. Go play footie with the Black kids down below,' his father used to say. Omar is painfully reminded of this, each May, when he drops his customers off at Roland-Garros. *A sport for rich kids.*

Omar has put his regrets behind him, reflecting that his case is far from isolated: the sport's reputation alone has probably prevented plenty of boys like Omar from joining a club. Same goes for golf and skiing.

Omar had no difficulty finding Nadia's profile or noticing that her social life was blatantly richer than his own. Her photos, which he took the trouble of scrolling through one by one, with the same moronic expression he displayed every time he thought about her, attracted plenty of

139

comments. He had a wobble when it came to sending her a message, his old self-destructive demons returning. Courage was decidedly not his number one attribute. But this time Omar managed to hold it together and write an unoriginal message asking for her news: 'Hi, it's Omar here, thanks for your kind comment on the app, how's it going?'

She replied the same day, flattered and enthusiastic, judging by the number of exclamation marks embellishing her answer.

They've been messaging each other for two or three weeks now, and it's a comfortable way to get to know one another, without being destabilised by smouldering eyes or a disconcerting perfume.

Omar could have carried on like that for weeks, content with the thrill of discovering an unread message in his Facebook notifications, revealing himself virtually, from the safe space of his studio bedroom, with his Lenovo IdeaPad 320S resting on the Formica coffee table picked up by Brahim at some flea market.

But while Omar is spraying the wheels of his Talisman with the high-pressure jet washer, he decides it's time to move up a gear. He glances around. *Hmm, weird, no sign of the Sri Lankan who offers to clean your car for a shitty 5 euros.*

The Talisman is spotless: it's time to hit the road and open the app. He's made up his mind that, this evening, after work, he'll send Nadia a message inviting her out for a drink or something to eat. He'll need to log into his Facebook account, password: Omar.kil.me. (He's chosen this infamous misspelling because Omar Raddad's case looks like it might be reopened, thirty years on. Will the illiterate Moroccan gardener finally be cleared of his boss's murder and mangling the French language in bloodstained letters?).

Just the thought of inviting Nadia out makes Omar smile gormlessly and switch on the radio, which is tuned to *Les Petites Annonces de Beur FM*, the phone-in show presented by Philippe Robichon. A woman in her fifties, Mimouna, is selling a 'villa' in Oran for 43,000 dinars: nine rooms, small hammam, courtyard and commercial premises. 'No time wasters, my brother's on site to arrange visits, I live in Bobigny, that's it, thanks, Philippe, and can I just say how much I love your show, by the way?'

Perhaps, one day, Omar will be able to buy his parents a *villa,* and that doesn't mean a luxury celeb pad in Santa Monica, no, by *villas* we're talking concrete boxes three storeys high, by the roadside back in the bled, with redbrick facades, unstable wrought-iron balconies and zellige tiles intended to make the place look like a Turkish palace.

If he's not going to become a tennis champion or realise his own dreams, Omar could at least make the more accessible dreams of his parents come true.

She knows only the president's name, François Mitterrand, and that he had campaigned to keep Algeria part of France, back in the day, so he was no friend. Yamina has never seen a sky so grey, or clouds so heavy, never known nights so cold.

Here she is. In France.

It was the best he could find, in a hurry. Brahim Taleb was finally bringing over his wife. His application for family reunification had been processed faster than expected, leaving him two weeks to organise accommodation. He had always lived alone until then, or with the other boys from the construction sites, in café-hotels, worker hostels, camps, prefabs and even a stint at his cousin's place in the shanty town of Nanterre, on his arrival in the Paris area in 1961. What sticks in his memory from that period is the filth, the shoes full of mud, the rats and the drumming on the zinc over his head. On rainy nights, getting to sleep was hell.

Brahim can't recall all the names of those who shared

the tin shack with him, it's a distant memory now.

But he does remember Nasser, who never came back. Another body, they said, dumped in the Seine by the French police.

A few of the boys from the old days had already returned to the home country, taking up the government's offer of the Voluntary Assisted Return Programme. This paid expulsion amounted to 10,000 francs.

Ten thousand pitiful francs for years of abject misery.

This 'aid' was a disgrace disguised as a favour, and Brahim understood that it meant: *We don't need your big hands anymore, your moustaches that freeze over in winter, we no longer need your self-denial, your nostalgic eyes, your sturdy legs, you take up too much room, even with your backs bent, and, as for the rest of your kind, what would we do with them? Those that come after you? For you flood over here and then you reproduce. It's time to go back to your villages and your ways.*

Ten thousand francs, scarcely the price of an honest thank you.

Sometimes, when he was weary of it all, Brahim dreamed of going home, but this would mean forgoing his years of service with his employer in the building and public works sector. He was middle-aged and it was too late to start over.

Thanks to his Kabyle comrades from the hostel at Puteaux, Brahim has found this one-bedroom apartment riddled with damp on rue du Moutier, in Aubervilliers. The landlord is called Monsieur Bonnet and he's warned Brahim that if any of the tenants in the building fall behind on the rent or the bills, he will cut off the water supply for everybody until he's been paid.

There may not be a shower in the apartment, but the toilet isn't on the landing, which is a start. Someone pointed out to Brahim the public baths on the corner of rue Paul Bert and rue Henri Barbusse. If he and his young wife go there once a week that should do the trick; they can make do with cold water straight from the kitchen tap for their daily ablutions. Washing in cold water never killed anyone: it's how Brahim has survived his entire life as a bachelor.

It's not as if his future wife is used to luxury, given that she, too, is from Msirda, born in the frontier zones, and raised on the farm with only basic comforts. Acclimatising to life here should come easily to her.

Brahim knows he'll be gentle with her. He won't hit her if she raises her voice, unlike some of his building site friends with their women. Brahim only listens with half an ear when they lecture him on how to treat women, since he doesn't believe in hagra – public humiliation – and he's not a violent man.

When he was younger, he refused to slit the throats of rabbits. It wasn't that he wimped out, but rather that his heart was tender, God had made him that way. It should also be added that his memories of the thrashings administered by his father ensured he never inflicted violence on a vulnerable being for the rest of his days.

Yamina hasn't stopped crying since she arrived here, despite Brahim's attempts to cheer her up. First, he buys her a radio-cassette player so she can listen to music when she's alone in the apartment from five in the morning until six o'clock at night. Next, he keeps offering her gifts of shoes and dresses purchased from Rosny-Prix on the Nationale 2, which may not be haute couture, but at the time he's the only man to give his wife shop-bought clothes.

He brings her fruit as well, to try to please her.

Once, he brings her medlars from the market, which give off a delicious aroma as soon as the paper bag is opened. But Yamina bursts into tears again when Brahim holds out one of the juicy fruit, because, of course, at Père Madouri's farm there's a row of medlar trees. Why didn't he think of that?

Instead of helping her to forget her sadness for a moment, he succeeds in plunging her back into familial melancholy, reminding her of how much she misses her father! Her father, her father! For there's only him, Baba, the only word in her mouth! There are days when Brahim loses his patience. 'If it makes you so sad to live here with me, then pack your bags,' he's felt the urge to tell her, on not a few occasions. 'I'll take you back to your father's home in Algeria!'

But he's never said this out loud, never. He feels too sorry for Yamina, and doesn't want to make her heartbreak any worse. He also knows, deep down, that Yamina would be tempted to answer: 'Yes! Take me back to my father's house, I can't bear this country any longer, with its grey sky and heavy clouds, I can't bear the loneliness another moment, these endless days, waiting for you to come home, I can't bear my tongue dying from being trapped inside my mouth, I can't bear my senseless saliva, I'm telling you, not being able to speak to anybody is killing me, and even if the radio plays all day long, I can't talk back to it.'

Brahim has taken to his young bride, she's so beautiful, so gentle and gracious, and as for her eyes, well! He's never seen eyes that colour before. Sometimes, when he's looking at her, he loses himself a little, in a moment of exquisite distraction...

Brahim's tender heart can't resist Yamina, it's as if he's been waiting for her all his life. For too long his heart has been shrivelled beneath the manly chest of this strapping formworker. One day, he hopes, she will also take to him, and learn to love him in her turn.

He's counting on the arrival of spring, on stepping out for walks with her on his days off, and he's counting on a clearer sky that might, perhaps, make exile more bearable for his wife.

MAXI TOYS
169 BOULEVARD MACDONALD, PARIS (75019)
FRANCE, 2019

She wasn't expecting to hold out this long, but, given the running costs of her studio-apartment, she has no choice. This year, once again, she'll be part of the Christmas sales team at Maxi Toys. (Maxi TOZ, yes, for real, so we're talking *fart* in Arabic, or *who gives a toss* in French. Which makes this megastore Maxi Who-Gives-A-Farting-Toss.)

At thirty-two, she already suffers from back problems, and restocking the shelves of the construction toys section isn't helping.

Imane can't take much more of the unpleasant top-down atmosphere or the constant pressure. She was hoping to quit her job as a 'qualified salesperson' at the beginning of October! Fat chance, given that she's flexing her independence by renting her own apartment and, as everyone knows, living in Paris 'proper' involves making sacrifices.

Living in Paris 'improper' involves making sacrifices too, just not the same ones.

Twenty square metres of living space costs her 850 euros

a month, bills included. Imane fibbed to her parents about the rent, she had to, she couldn't divulge such a brutal, grotesque figure. The sum is indecent, barely less than Brahim's pension. And given they weren't fans of her leaving home in the first place…

If she told the truth, their reflex would be to convert the rent into dinars. *What's with them always doing that? Where's the point?*

Eyes bulging, they would probably exclaim: 'What? 850 euros! That's 8.5 million!'

When you add zeros and talk in millions, it turns everything into a drama, as if paying 850 a month for a studio in the eighteenth arrondissement wasn't dramatic enough already.

'You do realise with 8.5 million you could rent at least seven apartments in Aïn Témouchent?'

Imane might fire back: 'So, what on earth d'you expect me to do in Aïn Témouchent?'

And her parents would offer, in their defence: 'We weren't asking you to go and live there, or not straight away. We were just comparing, that's all!'

As a subtle marker of her irritation, Imane might raise an eyebrow: 'Yeah, well Aïn Témouchent's nice and all, but it's not Paris, and Algeria's not France.'

She knows her mother hates it when she talks like that.

'I beg your pardon? Do you have a problem with Algeria? What about the respect you owe our million and a half martyrs?'

And Imane, who knows just how to bug Yamina, would sigh and quip: 'A million here, a million there, you only ever talk in millions.'

That would be the last straw for Yamina, prompting one of the sisters, Hannah, probably, yes, with her big open face, to turn up the pressure on Imane. Being the Lucky Luke of the family, ready to draw her revolver at the right moment, Hannah would say something along the lines of: 'Don't get smart with us, *you're only French on paper*, as Le Pen likes to remind us. The way you go on, anyone'd think you were called Nadine and grew up in Brittany. What has France ever done for you?'

And so, this episode might end badly, with Imane slamming the front door on her way out, though not so hard she couldn't pretend it was the wind if her father kicked up a fuss.

She'd catch some air towards rue Danielle Casanova, hands in fake fur jacket, €79.90, from Zara in Le Millénaire shopping centre, thinking once again that her family doesn't understand her. She can't shake off the feeling she's different from them. *And anyway, there's only room for my big sisters and Omar.*

Which explains why, to avoid things coming to a head, Imane chose to fly the nest, even if it was a messy business, even if she felt bad about letting her parents down, especially her father.

It's time to rise to the challenge now, having spent too long whining about her lack of freedom and independence. And if this means living on 265 euros a month, so be it. No more impulse purchases from Zara.

€1,115 take-home salary minus €850 rent, util. incl. = just over 2.5 million dinars.

Bottom line, Imane can't complain. She's free, she's Parisian and she's a millionaire.

WILAYAS OF ORAN (31)
AÏN TÉMOUCHENT (46) AND TLEMCEN (13)
ALGERIA, HOLIDAYS, 1990–2000

Yamina and Brahim had never considered the question of *leisure* when it came to educating their children. Theirs was the 'survival generation'.

As far as they were concerned, raising children was first and foremost a matter of making sure *they lacked for nothing*.

If the kids could eat their fill, if they were suitably clothed and went to sleep in the warm, then it was a case of mission accomplished. It never occurred to them to tune in to their children's emotions, to respect their personalities or nurture their creativity.

The generation of parents that crouches down to provide honey-toned explanations, while looking their child in the eye, would come much later. The 'well-being generation'. *We'd like to take this opportunity to thank Super Nanny for her invaluable advice. Rest in peace, Cathy Sarrai.*

And so it was that *holidays*, for the Talebs, didn't have the same meaning as for other people. They didn't involve sending the kids on organised trips abroad to learn about another country, or another culture, still less paying for them to visit the seaside or attend camp to make new friends.

No, come the summer they packed up luggage, excess luggage and kids, and headed for Algeria, via a well-trodden route: taxi from Aubervilliers to Orly airport, south terminal, then Air Algérie to Oran. For two months, they swept across the west of the country, stopping here and there to visit family. They came bearing gifts and stayed a few days each time, so as not to offend anybody.

First up, Oran, because the Talebs always landed at Oran Es-Sénia airport. This hadn't yet been named Ahmed Ben Bella international airport in tribute to the former president who disappeared.

They would spend the first week as the guests of M'hamed, Brahim's older brother, who, in Yamina's words, was *the best of the brothers.*

He still lived with his wife Sakina and their children on the seventeenth floor of the tallest block in Cité du Rond-Point, Bel-Air district, in the same sea-view apartment in which Yamina had spent four months before joining Brahim in France.

This was Malika's, Hannah's, Imane's and Omar's favourite part of the trip. They felt like they were having a proper holiday, connected with young people who shared their aspirations: namely, enjoying themselves and living freely. The city was resplendent, bathed in a light that exists nowhere else. Malika found historical relics at every street corner, while her cousins, thrilled by her curiosity, were only too pleased to answer her questions.

Out of all their uncles' and aunts' offspring, the cousins in Oran were the funniest and warmest. After dinner, they would take the Taleb children out for a stroll and to eat Italian ice cream on the corniche.

Hannah often wondered how those born and bred over there managed to pick out the newcomers with such ease.

'They always know we're from France, even if we disguise ourselves to look like them, even if we wear our cousins' clothes or a headscarf, even if we don't give the game away by speaking Arabic with an accent, they can spot us straight off! You'd think they had an immigrant detector!'

'Yes, but we recognise them in France! It's the same, isn't it?'

Omar put things in perspective.

Oran in summertime meant every night was party night: the sound of raï music in the street, the sight of successive wedding processions.

The Taleb offspring discovered the love songs of Cheb Hasni, who maintained his place in Algerian hearts despite having been assassinated a few years earlier.

'But if he was just a singer, if he wasn't involved in

politics, then why did they kill him?'

Nobody could provide Imane with a satisfactory answer.

Cousin Rafik shyly translated a few of the raï master's lyrics for the girls. Omar was less keen, but still, navigating the language of love made everyone laugh.

When the family went on a walkabout in the commercial quarter of Mdina Jdida, Malika noticed that the women were fashion-conscious and free, and most of the young people dressed in European style. The Taleb girls never felt uncomfortable here.

Sometimes, their eyes met those of other children of France, who were also figuring out how to fit in.

The weekend in Algeria meant Thursdays and Fridays. Everyone would set off for Plage Les Andalouses in the white Renault Trafic 2.5 van that belonged to Cousin Mohamed, who ran a transport company at the time.

The girls wore their gandouras to bathe, Omar his Bermuda shorts, Yamina sat under the parasol, and Brahim was happy to roll up his trouser bottoms and stand at the water's edge, his hands resting in the small of his back as he stared at the horizon. He was like an off-duty lifeguard, an incognito Mitch Buchannon from *Baywatch*. Only later did the siblings realise that their father had never learned to swim.

In the evenings, the cousins piled into the boys' middle

bedroom to watch comedy sketches by Moustapha Bilahoudoud on the state channel. Without subtitles, the Taleb offspring didn't get all the jokes, but the main ingredient was there: laughter.

They made a point of ending their stay with a photo opportunity at Fort of Santa-Cruz, built by the Spanish on an old Ottoman site where nobody ever tired of the view. 'It's so beautiful,' someone would venture, 'I can understand why the French didn't want to leave.'

A few years later Uncle M'hamed, may he rest in peace, died in his sixties, of a heart attack at the foot of his tower block at Cité du Rond-Point. Holidays in Oran were never the same again. Nor had they been since the beginning of the dramatic decade in which fear had seized the upper hand.

Every year, it was the same story: goodbyes that felt more like final farewells.

Next, the family made for Aïn Témouchent, sixty kilometres west of Oran, to stay with Yamina's parents, the Madouris.

In honour of the immigrants' arrival, Mohamed Madouri, the happy grandfather with his razza – a yellow satin turban – fixed to his head, would slit a sheep's throat. No debating animal suffering or empathising with the beast's lot: this was throat-slitting as an act of joy. The children argued about who was going to help Jeddi Mohamed hold the animal down. To bring matters to a head, and, above all, before severing the head, their grandfather used to say: 'Don't fight over it! There are four of you and, as it happens, this sheep has four legs!'

Omar was fascinated by the perfectly sharpened blade that reflected the July sunlight, while Hannah-the-reckless knelt on the sheep's legs, with a firm grip on its hind quarters, fearing nothing. Only Malika was sickened by the sight of blood.

They would immediately carve up the beast, washing the guts before cleaning the skin and wool, a task often undertaken by Yamina, whose expert reputation preceded her. At the same time, the aunties lit what they called *the tripod*, the gas ring to grill the liver, which, according to ritual, they ate first with a pinch of coarse salt.

One day blurred into another on the farm. Sometimes they ventured out, going from one house to the next, paying a visit to the home of one of the uncles or aunts, all of whom lived within a small radius, in the same administrative province, or wilaya, Aïn Témouchent (46).

Otherwise, the children played in the fields of wheat, with the kids from the farm staring at them as if they were specimens. 'They're weird, they're not like us,' Imane kept saying. 'How come it doesn't hurt when they walk barefoot over the stones?' The days were so long they lost all sense of time. Malika wrote postcards to her schoolfriends that she never got around to posting, but thrust into their hands on the first day back of the autumn term.

With their two young aunties, the ones who weren't

married yet, Malika, Hannah and Imane learned how to become proper little women. Summer chez Madouri was like a training programme for perfect wives-to-be. They wore gandouras, as well as headscarves tied at the back of the neck, Turkish style, and, in a colour of their choice, the inevitable *sandalas* or plastic beach shoes. They did the laundry by hand, in the sun, as well as peeling the vegetables, taking care of the hens, grilling the peppers and cleaning the courtyard with a small hand brush made from doum, the same palm leaf used for weaving baskets. In Algeria, the girls learned what was expected of a housewife. This included how to operate the Singer sewing machine that had long ago belonged to their mother before their Tata Norah took up the mantle.

Omar, whose good fortune it was to be a boy, accompanied his father into town, catching public buses whose ticket collectors were teenagers in sliders, then sitting at the cafés on the boulevard drinking dark-orange imitation Fanta. He was flexing the privilege of men and their freedom without realising it. He barely registered he was in another country.

One day, aged about eight, and staring at the people around him in the town centre, Omar noticed that everybody looked more or less alike, prompting him to ask his father: 'Papa, why are there only Arabs here?'

But not even he could escape the siesta imposed on everybody by the forty-degree afternoon heat, just after the Mexican telenovela, which was dubbed into Standard Arabic so that neither Omar nor his grandmother Rahma, who spoke only the Western Algerian dialect, could understand a word.

The girls didn't go out during their stay at Aïn Témouchent, where the mindset wasn't the same as in Oran. The town was populated by men. Theirs was the main boulevard, and the pavements belonged entirely to them: menfolk sitting on plastic chairs, spread across adjoining terraces that stretched all the way to the road.

They would stay there for hours, legs splayed, nude feet in foam sandals, talking loudly, smoking cheap Rym cigarettes, stroking their moustaches and nudging their Ray-Ban-inspired aviator sunglasses up the bridge of their noses. They sweated in their mandatory white vests, visible through their short-sleeved striped shirts.

Meanwhile, out on the boulevard, the women passed by as quickly as possible, furtive silhouettes, their bodies hidden beneath colourful djellabas.

It was up to the women to avoid *them*, the men.

To the point of stepping out into the road, at the risk of being run over, gripping the hands of their fragile sons in shorts as well as those of their young daughters, destined to pass fleetingly through these streets, just like their mothers.

These little girls were already finding out that women had to zigzag on the pavements, that it was up to them to be swift-footed, agile, up to them to play this game, to be inventive when it came to avoiding the men, to weave their way around the clumsy plastic chairs, around the clumsy legs splayed on those chairs, that the onus was on them to foil the plots, to dodge the clumsy moustaches ushering cigarette smoke, to dodge the clumsy chests beneath vests stained yellow by sweat.

Quicker than expected, young girls had to devise new itineraries, new methods of *passing without disturbing*.

Luckily for the Taleb girls, Fridays meant the weekly trip to the hammam, which they were all crazy about, apart from Imane, who couldn't handle the heat. One visit in two she fainted and had to be taken to the cooling-off room where she was laid out on a banquette, only to endure the brutality of the old kiyassa, ancient and vast-chested, who rubbed her down vigorously with a massage glove.

Once, at the hammam at Cité Thiers, a girl using a disposable man's razor to shave her thighs and arms asked if she could 'borrow' some of Imane's shower gel *from France*. Reluctant to share the caramel-scented bottle of Cottage, which had cost nearly 3 euros, Imane squirted two or three blobs into the girl's palm. In truth, she knew her hand was forced, as it always would be in this place where the other girls were forever filching from her. *I'm not surprised*, she thought, when one of her uncles informed her that Aïn Témouchent, in the Berber dialect, meant *watering hole of the jackals*.

Sometimes, it reached the level of racketeering.

Cousin Najat, who was a bit of a klepto, was always on the lookout for something to nab. It was exasperating, but they could never say no to her or she'd make a scene. In any case, either they gave it to her, or she helped herself. The girls had to keep tabs on their belongings and make an inventory of any missing items. Even Hannah, who was less restrained than the others, bit her lip and kept her mouth shut when her Helena Rubinstein Longlash Effect Mascara disappeared. They couldn't risk bringing shame on Yamina.

Malika's raspberry lip gloss suffered the same fate, but she wasn't too fussed, since it had come free with the July edition of *Glamour*, purchased from Relais H at Orly Sud airport on the outbound leg of their journey.

Still, enough was enough.

'Why do we have to zip it every time this happens? It's not our fault we were born in France, nobody consulted us about it. So how come we have to pay a jealousy tax?'

Imane was protesting the injustice of seeing the level of her Eau Jeune Démon go down day after day.

'Okay, so it's not Chanel, it's just a supermarket perfume, but it belongs to us, it's our bottle of perfume, doesn't it drive you crazy, we're not allowed any personal belongings here?'

She was hoping to corral her sisters into her rebellion.

The worst of it was that Najat didn't even try to be discreet about it, she just squirted herself with the perfume, spraying it all over her clothes and scarf before plonking herself next to Imane.

'Fuck's sake, she's taking the piss here, she knows I'll recognise the scent since it's, like, *mine*. She's triggering me, for real, I'm gonna smash her face in.'

Too right, Najat was thumbing her nose at them, because she knew that Imane, Hannah and Malika would be too embarrassed to complain, or else they'd get a roasting from their mother, and with good reason, seeing as Najat's cousins from France could buy as much perfume as they liked, because they'd been lucky enough to be born over there, and there was no arguing with it. Najat knew that although Brahim wasn't wealthy, he would always have more than her own father, who struggled to make it to the end of the month on his 3-million-dinar salary, and this despite his long service as a primary school teacher.

Najat had zero interest in her cousins' identity complexes or issues with systemic racism, and she barely listened when they talked about the kinds of discrimination suffered by the children of immigrants. She couldn't have cared less about their whingeing. All Najat knew was that they were the ones who got to wear Eau Jeune Démon, and not her.

Having looked forward all year to what the family teasingly referred to as 'her holidays', Yamina paid little attention to the girls' scrapping.

She was resolved to squeeze every drop of enjoyment out of seeing her parents, as well as her brothers and sisters, who, married or not, all lived close by. Yamina was making up for lost time. She loved gazing at her father. He might have aged, but his blue eyes still took her breath away.

When it was time for the daily ritual of drinking tea, he would emerge from the small garden behind the house and cut branches of fresh mint using his real-deal Laguiole knife, the one he had removed from the pocket of a French officer, captured in 1959. Mohamed Madouri prepared the tea himself, always taking care to serve Yamina first, in feeble and belated recognition of this daughter who, in his own words, *was worth all six sons put together.*

The Talebs' stay in Algeria always ended in the cradle, a return to their native land, Msirda Fouaga, close by the Moroccan border, in the place where Brahim's father, who had been the village imam back in the day, was buried.

It was some journey: four hours of burning the rubber in a public yellow Peugeot taxi, with a driver short on small talk. They would only stop once, for lunch at Maghnia and to buy spices. The grand souk was a temple, and Malika often photographed the stallholders with their mountains of colours.

The family at Msirda was diminished, with most members having migrated towards Oran in search of work. Fatima, Brahim's older sister, was the only one to have stayed in the area with her husband Abdelkader, their children and grandchildren. It was impossible to pin an age on Fatima, she was the archetypal female elder.

This meant that the Taleb children had a cousin of around

fifty, Sherif, who wore his moustache and hat with pride and his name like a dream. He was father to three grown-up sons as well as three nippers, who ran wild and peed everywhere.

There was no clock or mirror or television inside the traditional stone walls of Auntie Fatima's mechta. Time stood still, literally. Every day they ate the same food, sent by God: rye bread, olive oil, figs, eggs, tomatoes, peppers, Barbary figs that grew in abundance around the house, and boiled potatoes.

There was nothing for the young Talebs to do apart from sleep, walk, climb trees, catch beetles and ride for a few metres on the donkey. Nothing more stimulating.

They couldn't wait for evening to come, making sure to do their business before sundown, behind the cactuses, outside the mechta, in among the hens, to avoid an emergency trip in the middle of the night, because all the stories of vipers and jackals had scared them stiff. One problem: eating Barbary figs all day gives you diarrhoea.

Come nightfall, sitting on the esparto grass matting in the courtyard, everybody was in the thrall of their aged aunt. In the moonlight, with her tribal tattoos, hand gestures and husky voice, she was like an ogress from tales of bygone ages. Fatima was an ace at hijayat, the traditional tales and riddles told in rhyme. Malika wrote a few of them down in her jotter; she thought it would be a shame for them to vanish altogether. As for Hannah, the magic of those

Msirda evenings made her dream prematurely of her own old age and death: *I want to be buried here, not at Auber.*

Sometimes, at night, they could hear the clanking of jerrycans and the sound of their cousins coughing as they loaded up the old bottle-green Mercedes 190 E.

Msirda was the gateway to Morocco and, in order to survive, the sons of Uncle Sherif devoted themselves to trafficking cheap petrol from this side of the border. The Dalton cousins, as Hannah had dubbed them, sold fuel and stocked up on kief.

When they offered some smoke to Omar, who must have been twelve or thirteen, he declined, taken aback. The cousins called him a wimp. Offended, Omar stared at them thinking: *Look who's talking, with your eight teeth apiece.*

Not that he had the nerve to say this out loud.

For the first time, Omar reflected on what his life might have been if he hadn't been born in Aubervilliers, at the Roseraie General Clinic, AKA the butcher's of the 9.3 postcode, if his mother and father hadn't been exiles, and if they'd stayed here, in Algeria, on home soil.

Perhaps he too would have turned into a sixteen-year-old who looked thirty-nine. He too would probably have lost his teeth prematurely and driven the smugglers' roads by night.

That's destiny for you.

COMMUNE OF AUBERVILLIERS
DEPARTMENT OF SEINE-SAINT-DENIS (93300)
FRANCE, 2020

Hannah still feels ashamed about seeing a therapist. Once a week.

She hasn't told anyone.

She lets her parents, her brother and sisters think she's enrolled in Zumba classes, which to her mind is more socially acceptable.

It took forever for Hannah to embrace the process.

And she's not comfortable with it. Not yet.

To start with, she had to dismantle a heap of internal obstacles, knock down millions of oversized barriers.

First obstacle: *I'm not weak, I'm a fighter, like my mother, I'm Algerian, I stand on my own two feet, I don't need help.* Words that wouldn't have sounded out of place if she were raising her fist or waving the Algerian flag.

Contrary to what people say, that flag isn't an instrument of provocation but the embodiment of freedom won at the price of numerous sacrifices.

Hannah found it hard to admit that doing the work

on herself, to become a better individual, wasn't a sign of weakness.

The second obstacle, and it's a tough one, is of a spiritual nature: *I have my faith and I ask only God for help.* It took Hannah a while to understand that God might take the form of a psychologist in a chic consultation room in the eleventh arrondissement of Paris.

Plus, it pained her to spend money talking to a stranger about her *little troubles*.

Money which her father had earned the hard way, down the mine. She had a problem with the bourgeois image of a thirty-five-year-old woman, not especially unhappy, squishing her big bottom onto a teal-coloured Alinéa armchair, 430 euros, to ask herself a few existential questions. *This is ridiculous, for fuck's sake, yes, I've got one or two things to sort out, for sure, but we're not talking some horror story either, I haven't come from Auschwitz, or been tortured in the Congo, I've just got a few issues.*

And there you have it, it's here that she and her therapist must begin, with the biggest obstacle in Hannah's life, the question of *legitimacy*.

In her day job, Hannah frequently encounters psychologists; they're part of her team, which offers support to families. Hannah has been a youth worker for ten years, helping young people to retrain at Épinay-sur-Seine, dealing with parents caught in the poverty trap, kids who've dropped out, exhausted supervisors and teenagers who don't dream.

After ten years of risking her neck in this job, what saves her is the soul she puts into it.

Hannah has finally understood that, in order to help others, she must begin by helping herself. Conversations with a colleague have made her appreciate how important it is to talk to somebody who understands *who we are*, somebody who won't need everything explaining, or translating, or dissecting, when carrying this burden is exhausting enough. If she is to offload, Hannah needs a professional who will make things easier for her, *for once*.

And so, on a Wednesday in September, she goes to see Madame Aït Ahmad, boulevard Richard-Lenoir, 75011 Paris.

At the entrance to the consulting room, there's a huge painting of a Saharan landscape. Hannah finds the ochre of the dunes comforting, and it helps her to forget, for a moment, the sickening sense of betraying her own.

This guilt that weighs more heavily on her heart than a three-tonne truck on the asphalt of the A86.

To open up about her private life, to talk about herself, to lay bare her story, is, in her eyes, an admission of cowardice, proof she isn't up to dealing with it, when her pathetic bundle of personal worries doesn't represent a tenth of the burden borne by her mother, who has kept her silence, never complained and courageously overcome a life of challenges. Hannah feels ashamed, but something tells her that she must cross this frontier, if not for her own benefit, then perhaps for the children barely planned, not yet born, a blur; for them, she tells herself, she has to make peace.

Because her children won't know how to relate to this story. Experiencing *who we are* will only become more complicated, as what's unvoiced inside us becomes more difficult to unravel. Hannah is clear-headed about this, she understands that she can't always be incandescent.

Her parents strove to stifle this anger in themselves. They went to such pains to disguise it, to protect Hannah, her sisters and her brother.

And yet, for all that Yamina and Brahim tried to pretend everything was just fine, that you could overcome injustice without suffering consequences, there are cracks, however invisible, and these cracks are now in Hannah's flesh, burning her skin. And for all that she can't get the advertising jingle out of her head – 'Carglass repairs, Carglass replaces' – she knows that a crack on the windscreen is easier to fix than a shattered identity.

And if, one day, she finds some fool who's willing to give her kids, Hannah doesn't want them to inherit this anger that is eating her up inside.

Let them inherit their glorious history! The narrative of their struggles! Let them be proud of who they are!

They will know who Djamila Bouhired is, who Yamina and Brahim are, who Mohamed Madouri was, and his wife

Rahma, *peace be with them!* They will inherit the beauty of the poems recited under the stars at Msirda Fouaga, and perhaps, at last, they will be legitimate.

Hannah hopes that they, at least, won't have to keep fighting for it.

BOBIGNY REGISTRY OFFICE
31 AVENUE DU PRÉSIDENT SALVADOR ALLENDE
DEPARTMENT OF SEINE-SAINT-DENIS (93300)
FRANCE, 2020

As a registrar, pay band C, recruited through open competition, it's incumbent on Malika to represent the French state, embodying its neutrality.

But behind her desk, Pod A, on the first floor of Bobigny registry office, she can't always wash her hands of what she is in life. She struggles with the impartial distance she's required to maintain when dealing with the public.

Take this morning, the stammering old man with worn-out hands and cheap beret, tormented by words that won't come, by a language that eludes him, despite long years spent roaming this land. And so, once again, Malika steps out of role, she can't watch this chibani drowning in his words and not hold out a caring hand.

She knows she's not supposed to use Arabic with her clients, but this morning she switches back to her mother tongue so that the old man before her can make himself understood. Malika decides to liberate him, briefly, and the man's exhausted eyes light up when she addresses him in his dialect.

She has already received a ticking off about this.

Somebody snitched on Malika, and she thinks she knows who the culprit is: Bianca, her forty-something colleague from Martinique, who, in her refusal to deviate from a single unjust rule, surely dishonours the memory of her esteemed compatriot, Frantz Fanon. Malika has read the complete works of Fanon.

Although she's never confronted Bianca about it, this doesn't stop Malika from dwelling on the matter, or giving Bianca-the-informer a dirty look while refusing to answer her *bonjour*. 'No thanks,' she'd like to say, 'keep your coffee to yourself, traitor.'

Ever since Malika was summoned to explain her conduct, Bianca has made a show of being weirdly nice towards her. Malika hasn't said anything, but she views Bianca with contempt, much as she does her colleague's keenness to suck up to their manager, to be seen in a good light, to play the model student, and all for some worthless scrap of encouragement, some pathetic reward. She holds it against Bianca for not taking Malika's side when, normally speaking, she should understand, shouldn't she?

Why insist on making things harder for these people, when you have the means to help them? Malika doesn't consider what she's doing to be a violation of her public service duties; quite the opposite.

Over the ritual of Saturday lunch, she happened to mention

this incident at the family table, and Yamina wasn't at all happy about it. She didn't want Malika drawing attention to herself.

'You've just been taken on, the Mairie is a good job, binti, you've got it all, the computer, the chair, the heating, the payslips! Please, remember to be discreet!'

Hannah, as usual, was the first to let rip. She couldn't understand why her mother didn't support Malika in this matter, given that she couldn't abide injustice herself, and now, here she was, emphasising the need for discretion yet again.

'There are people who have died as a result of your discretion, isn't that enough for you? Haven't we been suitably discreet, as it is?'

'Is it written into your contract,' Omar said pragmatically, 'that it's forbidden to speak in Arabic with customers who can't get by in French?'

Malika was so happy to be employed by local government services that she hadn't bothered reading her contract carefully, and had signed on the spot.

'If the old man had been American, and you'd explained some things to him in English,' Imane suggested, 'I bet nobody would've minded.'

'For real!' Hannah agreed in her deep voice that sounded permanently exasperated. 'She'd probably have got a promotion!' And with that, she sank her teeth into a meat pie.

It's a calm morning on the first floor of the Mairie, nothing going on, except, perhaps, for this father of Turkish heritage who's come to declare the birth of his first child. So emotional is he that his eyes fill with tears as he slowly spells out to Malika his son's first name: 'Gürkan: G–Ü–R–K–A–N. It was my father's name,' he adds, 'it's a tribute to him, he died last year.' Malika is touched by the man's sensitivity. *What a pity guys like him are never single. The only ones left are heartless basket cases, but if that's what you're after, the streets are heaving with them.*

Fortunately, the individual pods at Bobigny registry office mean that Malika doesn't have to endure the lack of privacy that is open plan working. She can make the most of the lull to enjoy her secret weapon: power napping. The rest of the time, she reads her books or surfs the web, with no particular aim in mind.

Malika wonders if people still talk about surfing the web. It must be beyond retro by now, but she still says it. Then again, she can remember the arrival of ADSL, MSN Messenger and Lycos, the search engine with the black Labrador as its mascot. In the ad, a voice called out: 'Lycos, go get it!' or something to that effect. Malika couldn't say where the idea came from, but she starts typing 'village school of Sidi Ben Adda, 1964' into Google.

It'll be a nice surprise for her mother, she reckons, if she can track down some memories from Yamina's childhood in Algeria. Malika throws herself into exploring, pushing her files to one side. Too bad, she'll finish up later.

She begins by browsing a few sites, but nothing grabs her attention. It's all recent material, of little or no interest, photomontages of landscapes and the like.

Then she remembers that, back in the days of the French, Sidi Ben Adda was known by a different name; maybe she'd have more luck if she searched under Les Trois Marabouts. *That was the old name for the village, I think that's what Maman used to say.*

So, Malika types: Trois Marabouts village school, Algeria, 1964.

Every now and again, Yamina shares snippets from her childhood.

She talks about school, for the most part, telling her kids how much she loved going to school, and how she still remembers her primary school teacher, Madame Roque. When Malika was very young, and her mother used to speak affectionately about this Madame Roque, the little girl would picture a Madame ROCK, R-O-C-K, *rock 'n' roll*, dressed like Elvis Presley, wearing cowboy boots to teach French in an old colonial classroom.

Bingo. Malika lands on a blog, Friends of Les Trois Marabouts, with, at the top, the village insignia. Except that scarcely has she begun to scan the entries than she realises her mother is being exposed as a rotten liar.

Not a trace of Yamina or her childhood, none of the accounts she's given put in any appearance here, not one of her memories recorded. This is definitely *not* her mother's Algeria. In less than a second, Yamina has become Peter Pan, growing up in an imaginary faraway land, among the Lost Boys.

Malika scrolls through all the different sections, but she can't find anything, not a jot, not a single encouraging detail.

There are plenty of images of what used to be the Mairie, of a postal wagon travelling through the trees, along the route de la Pepinière, a photo of a rural home and stone washhouse, the carefree youths of Les Trois Marabouts enjoying the beach, a comprehensive list detailing the names of the different plumbers, butchers, market gardeners, tenant farmers and milkmen who plied their trades in and around the village for decades.

You can even find out about its last annual fête, in 1954, when the village was honoured by special guest Mendizabal, *doyen of tango and virtuoso of the bandonéon.* Fat help that is for Malika, who has to open a new window to look it up. *Bandonéon? Aha! So that's what it is! Like those small accordions the Roma play on the métro, Line 5!*

Malika is in awe of these people preserving their memories. The Friends of Les Trois Marabouts even organised a pilgrimage to the region of Aïn Témouchent, back in 2013.

Pieds-Noirs retracing the colonial days of their youth. She reads their travel journal and looks at everything they've posted under the heading: TO END OUR 'NOSTALGERIA', A SUCCESSFUL RETURN TO THE AREA! They miss the village church, which has been transformed into a mosque, but still, keen to keep the tone upbeat, they write: *A country rebuilding itself! A long way to go before it becomes a 'tourist attraction', but they're working on it!*

Malika is astonished to read all of this.

She didn't realise how much they, unlike her, her sisters and her brother, *felt at home* over there. She almost envies them, *it must be nice, just once, to feel at home* somewhere.

In the class photos of 1964 unearthed by the writers of the blog, Malika stares at the little girls, all stiff, in black and white, in the absurd hope of finding, among all these faces, her mother's. Perhaps, in the blur of so many surnames, Gimenez, Navarro, Lopez and Bensoussan, she will land on the surname that belongs to Yamina: Madouri, M-A-D-O-U-R-I, this name which also deserves to be written down, to be recorded in a register, this name which also deserves to be remembered and to be spoken out loud with emotion.

It would have meant so much to Malika to be able to recognise her mother, her innocence, her honey-coloured eyes, in one of these photographs. But, by then, Yamina would have been taken out of school.

Malika will never know what her mother looked like

before she was thirty, before that identity photograph taken for her passport in 1981 ahead of her arrival in France, in which she wears her broken-hearted expression and big fake mink collar, which was all the rage at the time.

Through details recorded meticulously by the blog's authors, Malika learns a fair amount about the history of Les Trois Marabouts: the dates, names and places, the ties and marriage alliances between the different families. She is impressed by their diligence in keeping hold of all *the proof* of their lives.

They've even posted a reproduction of the first registry office certificate issued in the village: *a death certificate dated 1881*. As if the man named were *the first man to die on that land*.

Malika feels a rush of sadness, there's something muted, deep inside her; it's as if she's realising, for the first time, that her ancestors, since there is no mention of them anywhere, never existed.

And this, in turn, makes her see herself as a ghost, descended from a long line of ghosts, even though Malika knows these ancestors of hers did exist, categorically existed, and their history is real, categorically real.

It's just that nobody took the trouble to write down this story of theirs, nobody made a note of their names, nobody assigned dates, nobody counted their living or their dead, especially not their dead.

They weren't photographed, all smiles, in front of their homes, with their children and their hopes, because, quite simply, all that had been confiscated.

Their lives were discreetly scattered in the dust.

And so, they must make do with a fragmented history, with these shards of memory.

Today, Malika understands that her inheritance is a jigsaw.

And even if Yamina has done her best to hand down some of the fragments, it's up to her children now, it's up to Malika and the others, to reassemble them.

BAR JOSEPHINE
45 BOULEVARD RASPAIL, PARIS (75006)
FRANCE, 2020

Omar can't stop wiping his clammy hands on his jeans, Celio Regular C5, W42. He's made the effort to dust off his suede shoes, the pair he's only worn once, back in 2015, for the wedding of Hassan Benahia, a guy from his class at Collège Gabriel Péri, who's missing two fingers, stupidly waylaid during his joinery apprenticeship.

His shoes could pass for new.

Omar also wears a shirt from Zara, decent cut, freshly ironed and smelling of Lenor Blue Spring Awakening, Yamina's favourite fabric conditioner.

Merci, Maman, oh man, what would I do without her?

Omar has checked the bar's website and the dress code is clearly stated as lounge suit: hello, it's not like he was planning to show up in his Bayern Munich tracksuit and 40-euro Reebok Royal Ultras from Go Sport. The website further stipulates: *Dogs under 10 kilos are welcome.* Phew, that's a relief.

So, Omar has finally decided to visit the Lutetia.

He's arranged to meet Nadia here this evening.

He enters the palace like a suspect, his face apologetic, his eyes saying sorry for the affront, begging forgiveness ahead of time. He enters the Lutetia with his poor man's mug and the manners to go with it.

'Good evening, monsieur, welcome!'

When the doorman greets him politely at the main entrance, Omar wants to turn on his heels. He's never felt so out of place in his entire life. *This is weird, it feels like a trap.*

Omar walks through the sumptuous lobby, barely taking in the spectacle, advancing warily, one foot in front of the other, as paranoid as Henry Hill at the end of *Goodfellas*, his favourite film, as if he was expecting to trigger an alarm, set off a metal detector, or activate a barrier, convinced he'll get caught in a security check. *Surely, they're not going to let me through this easily?*

Before getting out of the car, he checked he had his ID. That's the *Aubervilliers reflex*, always be ready to flash your papers, *big up to the BAC,* the anti-criminality brigade.

It's as if Omar is ready to be unmasked, expecting someone to call out: 'Grab him! He's an impostor!'

Omar tries to clamber inside another character's head, to man up, play a role that forces him to look confident, but this has the opposite effect. He figures he's about as composed as Billy, the irritating young American who stashes drugs under his civvies, sweating buckets before the Turkish customs officers rumble him, at the beginning of *Midnight Express*.

Omar has quite the film collection, thanks to his illegal downloads.

Bar Josephine is resplendent. Omar, who's out of breath, has just clocked from the decor that the bar's name is a tribute to Josephine Baker, who was a loyal customer of the Lutetia. Wow, he wasn't expecting that. She was Black, right?

He likes her song, 'J'ai deux amours'. Something in it speaks to Omar, the lyrics resonate.

> *On dit qu'au-delà des mers*
> *Là-bas sous le ciel clair*
> *Il existe une cité*
> *Au séjour enchanté*
> *Et sous les grands arbres noirs*
> *Chaque soir*
> *Vers elle s'en va tout mon espoir*
> *J'ai deux amours*
> *Mon pays et Paris*
> *Par eux toujours*
> *Mon cœur est ravi*

> *They say beyond the seas,*
> *Beneath the pale sky,*

There lies a city,
Of enchanted stay,
And under the tall dark trees,
Each evening,
My hopes head that way.
I have two loves
My country and Paris.
My heart by them is
forever ravished.

But he's not thinking about Manhattan.

For Omar, it's more a case of Algeria and Paris: '*J'ai deux amouuuurs, l'Algérie et Pariiiiis.*' Why's nobody ever thought of doing a remake?

Nobody asked Josephine to choose between her two loves, and she wasn't threatened with being stripped of her nationality, either.

While he waits for Nadia, Omar orders a drink. Full disclosure, the waiter hands him a menu in English, which Omar finds strangely flattering.

He spots the 'alcohol free' section and orders the least expensive cocktail, without bothering to check the ingredients. *Well, by 'least expensive', we're still talking 21 euros, and they even have the nerve to put the number of centilitres next to the price: fourteen! Shit, twenty-one readies for 14 cl, they're not messing about are they? So deal with it, big boy, don't look surprised... But €1.50 per centilitre? I mean, WTF! That's the price of a 33 cl can of Coke from the bakery at Fort d'Auber. Look, just stop comparing, this is nuts, behaving like your old man.*

It turns out he's chosen a cocktail named after another of Josephine's songs: 'Je ne veux pas travailler'. He's on the verge of switching drinks: *gonna come across too 'lazy Arab' if I order that.* He'd be lowering the tone of the cocktail. In Omar's mouth 'I don't want to work' makes him sound like a benefits scrounger, but, given the prices of the other cocktails, he sticks with his first choice.

Omar sips his drink very slowly.

He casts an eye over the food menu, just in case. If things go well with Nadia and the evening carries on, she's bound to get hungry. *Thirty euros for eight crab maki, twenty-four for the cheeseboard, eighteen for the salmon rillettes with sourdough.*

Omar hardly dares convert that into Uber trips. He has the same reflex as Brahim, except his currency is Ubers, not dinars. *Fifty-four euros, so that's a rush hour trip from Porte de Bagnolet to Orly West Terminal. Right, got it, inshallah she's not hungry.*

Omar smiles, he doesn't know why, remembering that time at a birthday party, music full blast, when he was talking to this girl, and they were both shouting to make themselves heard. They looked kind of stupid, as everybody does in that situation, and she asked him: 'What's your line of work?' He replied: 'I'm Uber, me,' so she said: 'Oh, right, sorry, yeah, we didn't introduce ourselves, pleased to meet you, Rupert, I'm Amal. It's funny, you don't look like a Rupert.'

Nadia finally makes her entrance. There's no denying the elegant figure she cuts in that slinky dress from H&M, €24.90 in a recent sale, though you'd swear it was a designer piece. Those charcoal eyes would make Josephine Baker lower hers in a staring match.

Omar's head is spinning from this dramatic arrival.

The way she walks across the bar, weaving between the tables, lets you know that Nadia, for one, has shrugged off all hang-ups. She doesn't want anybody debating *her place in the world*.

No two ways about it, Omar's fallen for this girl.

As Nadia apologises for being late and kisses him on the cheek, he's reminded of childhood trips to the cinema with his sisters, her scent a blend of candyfloss and caramelised popcorn.

She looks around her and cracks a couple of witty one-liners about the uptight customers and the Botoxed face of the Russian woman sitting nearby. Then she scrolls through the cocktail menu, raises an eyebrow and stares at Omar's glass, which is now empty.

'If you've finished, we don't have to stay you know.'

'Don't you like it here?' Omar asks, caught off guard.

Of course she likes it here, it's beautiful, but 'Hel-lo, they're having a laugh, right?' She smiles at Omar, puts her hand on his knee. 'I'm going to set you straight, from the get-go, you don't have to put on a show for me, I don't care about being impressed, plus I'm starving, I didn't have time for lunch, and we're not going to pay 24 euros for six codfish fritters. So come on, let's go.'

Omar feels uncomfortable about walking out. It was hard enough walking in, and leaving the Lutetia is going to be just as difficult. 'Are you sure? Can we really do that?' Nadia stands up, puts her jacket back on and bursts out laughing. 'We'll raise a few eyebrows, and…!'

Omar and Nadia leave the Lutetia to spend the rest of their evening at a Lebanese delicatessen that's much more relaxed.

He's understood that *she*'s the one, having always found love stories to be absurd before her, always thought he was ugly before she looked at him in that way, and now, here he is, someone who is starting to exist beyond the approving gaze of Yamina.

This evening, Omar's chin is up; he can love a woman at last, he can show himself for who he really is and expect love in return. It wasn't about *timing*, Omar realises, or *experience*, or *luck*, it was just about waiting to find *her*.

ORAL AND MAXILLOFACIAL CLINIC
PITIÉ-SALPÊTRIÈRE HOSPITAL
PARIS (75013)
FRANCE, 2020

Imane is a dab hand when it comes to avoidance tactics. She has delayed having her wisdom tooth out, number twenty-eight, until it's pushing its expiry date.

Now that it's touching the nerve and she can't sleep at night, she has no choice. Dosing up on a thousand milligrams of paracetamol and ibuprofen is about as effective as sucking on a sweet.

She had to make an emergency appointment at the Salpêtrière minor surgery clinic, where the oral surgeons have a decent reputation. Imane boasts a low pain threshold, and what she's dreading most is the injection in her jaw for the local anaesthetic. Even now, at thirty-three, she still needs her mother by her side when she goes to the dentist.

When one of Yamina's children reaches out for support, she always says, 'I'll be there,' and today was no exception. They crossed Paris together, Line 7, as far as Gare de l'Est, then Line 5 to Saint-Marcel, even though Yamina, who is sensitive to smells, often feels sick in the métro and prefers to take the bus on her rare trips into town.

But she's made the effort for Imane with the help of her little rollerball tube of musk, dabbing it on her wrists and sniffing them regularly to counter the nausea.

It's the beginning of the afternoon, mid-week, and there aren't many people in the waiting room.

Imane has taken annual leave, half a day that was a nightmare to get signed off, you'd think the manager of Maxi Toys had it in for her personally, deliberately giving her a hard time. She's forever trying to catch Imane out, always after her, watching over her, setting the stopwatch on her breaks, and balking when Imane is rash enough to ask for a day off.

Imane sees symbolism everywhere and believes in the body keeping the score: *This is down to her, because she's fed up to the back teeth with me.*

Yamina hasn't yet come to terms with Imane no longer living at home.

'If you still lived with us, I could take care of you, cook you up some soup... Are you sure you don't want to come back for a few days after the operation, until you're better?'

'I don't know, we'll see.'

Imane's answer is the equivalent of her mother's *inshallah*, which exasperated her when she was younger.

If God wills it so, that's something we can never know.

Imane's anxiety levels are rising, the wait's been twenty minutes already and there's panic setting in.

To cheer up her youngest daughter, Yamina starts describing her first tooth extraction, back in the days when her family were refugees in Morocco.

'Oh no, Maman! Not the story about the tooth puller, please, it's really not the time or place!'

It always begins like this: 'I've given birth to four children, but I've never been in as much pain as I was that day. There was no anaesthetic, no sterilisation, no antibiotics, no nothing…'

DOCTOR AÏT AHMAD'S PRACTICE
BOULEVARD RICHARD-LENOIR
PARIS (75011)
FRANCE, 2020

So, I'm sitting at a table in the Peking Express, well, it's called something else these days, the restaurant got bought up, but back then it was the Peking Express, one of the first halal Chinese restaurants, not far from the police station, and, I remember, they made delicious beef fried noodles. I'm telling you about this now, but I used to go there back in 2009, 2010, so it's old, right? I don't even know why I dreamed about the place. Anyway, I'm there with my friends, the lycée girls I haven't seen in years, we're together, having a laugh, eating stir-fried noodles and stuffing our faces with spring rolls. It's a feast, we've got these pyramids of spring rolls on the table. We're cracking out the jokes, chillin', enjoying the vibe.

Then come the noises, sirens, the screeching of tyres. We see this, like, CRS convoy, riot police vans parking up in front of the restaurant. I notice everyone starting to panic, I can see Sofiane, the owner, terrified, whipping out his hair clippers from under the till. He plugs them in and starts shaving his beard, because, and I remember this, Sofiane was one of the first to grow a beard back then. I'm watching him set to and he's shaving like a man possessed, he's bleeding, tufts of beard tumbling into the wok in front of him.

The other customers scramble to their feet and run for it, some hide under the tables, I've got no idea what's going on. 'Hey, what are you doing?' I ask Sofiane. 'Stop it! Why are you doing that?'

And I can see that he's crying while he's shaving, he's petrified.

That's when the riot police make their brutal entrance, kicking down the door, we can't make out their faces, they're wearing masks, like the special services. They're firing into the air and one of them's shouting: 'Down on the ground! Hands on your heads!' So, I get down.

There's this woman close to me, with a white headscarf, she's lying down as well, her hands over her head, and then she turns and I realise it's my mother, and she looks at me and goes 'Shh!', holding her finger to her mouth, and I say: 'But Maman, why do we have to shush? We haven't done anything!'

The cops start laying into the guys in the restaurant, their colleagues put Sofiane in a hammerlock, handcuff him and take him away. I can see they're hurting him.

Next, the ranks of soldiers arrive, top brass, nothing but old men, stacks of medals pinned to their chests. They've got sub-machine guns and they're aiming at us. The first old man is Jean-Marie Le Pen, but not the Le Pen from now, no, the Le Pen from before, from the eighties, with his pirate's headband. I can see him cackling, all buzzed up. He starts letting fly with the bullets, firing on the kids, any kid, in the head, point blank range, like in a video game, there's blood spurting everywhere, he's papping three or four kids at a time.

I'm still down on the ground, scared witless, I don't understand any of this. I look at my mother, who's reciting the Quran so softly it's like she's whispering.

And that's when the second old man moves in on her, he crouches down and places his knee on her skull, grinding her head into the ground so she can hardly breathe. I'm staring at the old man's face and I recognise General Aussaresses, with that eyepatch thingy of his, the one who tortured people during the Algerian War and went on to talk about it on the telly, defending his actions right up until his death, and I see him crushing Maman and I start to shout: 'Let her go!' I'm shouting with all my might: 'Let my mother go!'

And what does he do? He fixes me with his one eye, still grinding my mother's head into the ground, and he says to me with a smile: 'I've come to finish off the job.' He fires straight at me. Boom.

Every child has different monsters.

This is Hannah's fourth session with the therapist.

Her nightmares are something she talks about a great deal.

She warmed instantly to Doctor Aït Ahmad, confident she could trust her, *it's clear that she understands everything.*

Hannah frequently dreams about drowning, as well.

She might be struggling in the freezing waters of the Seine, while hordes of corpses float lifelessly around her, hundreds of men, their heads below the surface. Every time she turns a corpse over to identify it, she realises that it's her father and his face is being erased. She tries to rescue him, to get him out of the river, before his face has been erased altogether, but she's not a strong swimmer herself, so, by the time she's flailed over to the riverbank, it's too late, his face has been entirely rubbed out, and it always ends this way.

What's she meant to do with all these stories that haunt her? *The Algerian War, the Paris massacre of 17 October 1961 when the bodies of so many civilian Algerians ended up in the Seine, the anti-Arab beatings, the riots, the police blunders, people at work telling her about the ID checks gone wrong.* What's she meant to do with this feeling that history is repeating itself?

Hannah knows she is *particularly sensitive*; she's forever having people tell her how sensitive or impulsive she is. And she knows, too, that she's the first to pay for this heat, this immeasurable anger which rises up inside her.

Yes, she'd like to learn how to tame it, but the violence doesn't come from nowhere, and nor are the images in her nightmares ones she's made up, all this existed, and it still exists.

It does her good to hear the therapist's words: 'What you're experiencing is normal, this violence is part of your history, you carry within you the violence and humiliations experienced before you, you inherit them. It's normal for you to feel angry, it's an anger that has been repressed for so long, it's unjust, all of this, and injustice, by its nature, makes us profoundly angry.

'But you cannot carry the weight of all this alone. You cannot make reparations for the offence by yourself.'

Make reparations for the offence.

The words resonate for Hannah, they're like a revelation. At last, she has some words for it.

She has always sensed that she must make reparations for the offence endured by her parents. And what Hannah can't abide is the idea that, one day, they will be buried without having known the recognition they deserve.

If she doesn't undertake to do this, who will?

COMMUNE OF AUBERVILLIERS
DEPARTMENT OF SEINE–SAINT–DENIS (93300)
FRANCE, 2020

Brahim Taleb is a surprising man. Not a year goes by without him offering Yamina flowers on Valentine's Day. The bouquet of choice is eighteen red roses from Hana Flor, the Chinese florist on avenue de la République, next to the Roseraie General Clinic (AKA the butcher's of the 9.3 postcode).

And every year, a flustered Yamina says to her husband: 'Why are you parting with your money? It's a French celebration! Not for the likes of us!' But Brahim enjoys pleasing his wife, and he knows Yamina too well, so, yes, she always gives the same retort, but it doesn't escape his notice that she blushes, preens herself and hurries to arrange the flowers in a vase, after which she's all sweetness and light towards him.

From time to time, he slides a 20 euro note into the pages of her Quran, for her to treat herself to some trinkets at the market. Yamina discovers the note at dawn, when she's immersed in reading the verses of surah 18, Al-Kahf. She smiles, and melts.

Not that Brahim's efforts are entirely disinterested: he adores receiving compliments from the daughters in whom Yamina confides everything. They smother him with kisses to thank him for the kindnesses he shows their mother and to remind him that *he's the best*. They're proud to have *a romantic old man*. It's not common currency.

Hannah always boasts about this to her girlfriends: 'It's beyond cute, my dad's such a softie at heart.'

A man of Brahim's generation, the son of an Algerian countryman, born in the 1930s, a man of the mines, of working men's hostels and construction sites, isn't supposed to be tender or in love with his wife. He isn't supposed to give her red roses or lilies, or to ask his children to *tighten their belts*, so they can save up to buy a nice present for their mother's birthday, such as jewellery or perfume.

Brahim can't always find the right words, he can be grumpy at times, and he's always hungry, but he's a top-notch husband.

The children have never heard Brahim raise his voice against their mother. He hasn't been unfaithful, never had a second wife back in the bled, no half-Breton child ringing the doorbell aged eighteen to be reunited with his papa.

Brahim has always aspired to the quiet life, and his comfort resides in Yamina's heart.

Yamina eventually came around to loving him, this man

with his awkward manners, his moustache, his gruff voice, his baseball shoes, size forty-two with Velcro straps. Yamina can't understand a grown man wearing shoes with Velcro straps any more than Brahim can understand people wasting so much time tying up laces. She learned to love the way he snaps his fingers when he laughs, his oversized jackets, even his heavy smoker's habits and fondness for a flutter on the horses.

With his wife's encouragement, Brahim quit the cigarettes at sixty-three. One morning, he deposited his packet of no-filter Gauloises on the television, and it stayed there for several days without him touching the contents. He faced down the blue packet for almost a week, then, when he felt ready, he tossed it in the bin, ditching the bookies too while he was at it.

Not that this stops him from enjoying his little pleasures: dabbing on perfume (the same for forty years: Rêve d'Or), drinking a café crème at the Casanova on avenue Jean Jaurès, listening to his Dahmane El Harrachi cassettes, watching westerns on television, and, let's not forget, sitting down for mealtimes, because Brahim loves getting stuck in to his food.

So, how do you expect Malika, Hannah and Imane to get married?

Compared to their father, all the other men out there are wasters.

He's sitting in front of her, crying, and we're not talking a few tears shed with dignity. No, he's blubbing, close to suffocating. He's staring into the void, like he's just discovered his mother's corpse hanging in the loft.

'I don't understand,' he punctuates his sobs, 'I don't get it, I thought, you know, I felt like we had something strong between us.'

Imane watches in shock, aghast a person can lack pride to this extent. She feels no compassion whatsoever, level zero of empathy. This lack of masculinity bothers her, much as it does her sister Hannah. *I mean, if there's a war in France tomorrow, we're off to a bad start with basket cases like him.*

She thought she'd been clear when she said to Thomas, just as she had done to all the others: 'I'm warning you, no point in getting your hopes up, I won't commit.'

There's plenty for Imane to complain about when it comes to her relationships with Arab men. Sometimes, she despises their outdated thinking, their authority, the ease with which they get served, or their macho habits. But, at thirty-three years old, she's understood that she prefers an excess of masculinity to a deficit. She's appalled to witness Thomas bawling his eyes out in her studio-living room and crossing his legs like Sharon Stone in *Basic Instinct.* *Enough already with the white boy fragility*, she fumes. *It's like this whitey, this aspirin, this toubab* — and she flips the Wolof word into backslang — *this* babtou *is doing a live remake, just for my benefit.* Babtou Instinct.

And another thing, he's sitting there with his trainers on, which does Imane's head in. He never takes his shoes off when he's round at hers. *Fuck's sake, I mean, you shouldn't have to explain this kind of thing, right...?* Would she need to explain it to a Japanese guy?

She's not keen on him leaving his bottle of wine in her fridge, either, or making sarcastic remarks about religion. On the plus side, Thomas is kind, good-natured, easy-going and they never argue.

What delayed his fall from grace was his super-attentiveness. He cooked her delicious meals, took her out dancing, plied her with compliments and never succumbed to fits of jealousy. Trouble was, he flatlined. There was nothing *special* going down between them, and Imane couldn't bring herself to admire him.

Their story went up in a puff of smoke when a guy in a bar picked a quarrel with him. Imane watched Thomas shrinking, lowering his gaze, apologising: *he was scared of getting into a fight.*

She went right off him, on the spot, felt too ashamed to let him walk next to her. She no longer wanted to look him in the face, so she dumped him and headed home, switching off her phone, ignoring the dozens of text messages he sent through the night.

It was the same when it came to his relationship with money, *each for themselves and God for all,* always counting everything, contributing precisely his share, no more, no less, the exact change, always *let's split it down the middle, easy-peasy, right?*

Not that he needs to budget carefully, unlike Imane who's constantly overdrawn, because Thomas earns a fat whack, thank you, and, at thirty-five, already owns his apartment (which used to belong to his grandma, before she departed this life right on cue). How many times has Imane thought to herself: *He's not such a Mr Nice Guy, after all, or he wouldn't let me sweat blood like this.* As she watches him blubbing, what goes through her head is: *Fuck's sake, he hasn't even got a face, this guy, how did I ever give him the time of day? Working himself up into such a state after a two-month relationship… What would've happened if we'd stayed together for two years? He'd have slit his wrists in the bathtub!*

Imane reaches the sorry conclusion that she's too much of an outlier to find her match. She'll end up with a dozen ridiculously named cats who will help her overcome her loneliness and moult on her black polo necks.

Too independent for some. Not enough for others. She supports freedom of expression but isn't pro-*Charlie Hebdo* either. She is Muslim and feminist. She is French and Algerian. Her hair is neither straight nor curly. She's vegan when the food isn't halal. She is modern and reactionary. She is everything and its opposite.

Imane lives in a world which isn't yet ready to welcome her in all her complexity.

COMMUNE OF AUBERVILLIERS
DEPARTMENT OF SEINE–SAINT–DENIS (93300)
FRANCE, 2012/2015/2016

Oh no. Not that. Not again.

Like so many other French Muslim families, the Talebs clutch their foreheads, wild-eyed, before the appalling images and rolling news banners on the screen. It's almost beyond belief, and yet they're starting to become accustomed to this.

After the horror, the empathy for the victims and their families, the fear, the grief and all that a citizen who isn't devoid of humanity might feel comes the questioning. And the over-hasty thinking.

Please let it not be an 'Arab'. This is the secret wish of all the Taleb children.

They already know they'll be swiftly sidelined from the national mourning.

Once again, it will be confiscated from them.

Scarcely do they have time to register the tragedy, which has sometimes taken place under their noses, in Saint-Denis, scarcely time to emerge from their state of shock, scarcely time to comprehend the madness, then they're positioned on the side of the accused.

And so comes the moment of *disassociating*.

They will be asked, officially asked, to go out into the streets but in a separate procession, as a gathering of those 'of Muslim appearance' who wish to let it be known: *Don't be alarmed, we're not like them.*

There is no *instruction manual for peace-loving Muslims,* no guide to FNAC store protocol on *how to disassociate in the event of a terrorist attack.*

For the Talebs, as for all the others, there are no rules. If being affected as a human being and a citizen isn't deemed convincing enough, then what are they meant to do? Assimilate? Proclaim their French identity more robustly? Sing the Marseillaise more loudly? Change their given name? Sign up to an extreme right-wing party to earn unequivocal legitimacy? When will they ever be above and beyond suspicion? *And anyway, isn't aspiring to such a position even more suspect?*

This is what the Taleb children discuss around the table over Saturday lunch.

It's always Hannah who settles the matter. 'I mean, it

stands to reason, when you're legitimately French, you shouldn't have to prove it, time and time again!'

And yet they know they must prove their credentials, for this is what is required of them, this stupid injunction, immediately slapped on them, when emotions are still raw: *Disassociate yourselves from them.* Politicians, philosophers and journalists all calling on Muslims to rise from the ranks.

The Talebs, like so many other families, do not share the terrorists' beliefs.

The matter is self-evident as far as they're concerned. They have nothing in common with these monsters, aside from their *foreign-sounding* surnames and resident-alien features, since, unlike their history, their outsider faces refuse to be erased.

An undivided nation doesn't split off to mourn its dead.

That should be the true marker of unity.

COMMUNE OF PILLAC
DEPARTMENT OF CHARENTE (16390)
FRANCE, 2020

Five hundred kilometres and five hundred metres separate
Aubervilliers, Seine-Saint-Denis from Pillac in the
Charente, but, for the Talebs, the distance they're covering
is much more significant. It's not just about numbers or
geographical alignment, no, a whole world lies between
them and Pillac, in Nouvelle-Aquitaine.

For the first time ever, Yamina and Brahim are allowing
themselves *a real holiday*. This year, they're taking a break
from the ritual of their *annual leave as exiles*, which has
been unswervingly the same for forty years.

Since the death of their grandparents, some of the uncles
and great-aunts, as well as the general dispersing of the
family, their heart is no longer in it. Yamina has never fully
recovered from the death of her father, handsome Mohamed
Madouri, who suffered a stroke a few years back. Nor did
her mother Rahma tarry in following her husband, as was
her way, so Yamina lost both parents a few months apart.

She travelled alone to her father's burial, but, despite her daughters' best efforts to secure an emergency plane ticket, they didn't succeed in booking her on a flight in time for her father's interment. When the plane landed, the body of Mohamed Madouri had already been lowered into the ground and Yamina was inconsolable at not arriving early enough to gaze on his face one last time.

If only she didn't live in this accursed country, so far from kith and kin, especially her sisters and brothers, she would have enjoyed her father's presence more often, and, perhaps, had the good fortune to wish him a final farewell.

Briefly, on that day, she gave herself permission to rail in anger against France, against exile and its collateral damage.

Yamina and Brahim's offspring had opted out of the trips back to Algeria some while ago, or, at least, the four of them ceased joining their parents en masse. They chose instead to go away with friends, booking all-inclusive holidays in Turkey or road trips across the United States, as Hannah had the previous year.

It was Malika's idea to book a fortnight's holiday on Locasun.fr. She found a contender in the website's flash sale while 'surfing the web' at her desk, Pod A, Bobigny registry office.

Pillac, house, 8 people, 4 bedrooms, 170m², fully equipped kitchen, terrace, garden furniture, barbecue, private pool, ping-pong, swing.

'It's 700 euros a week,' Malika told her brother and sisters, 'and we can all chip in.' Imane, who didn't have the money, asked Omar to advance her share. 'Seven hundred euros!' Brahim pointed out. 'That makes it 7 million dinars!'

So, it's costing them less than 300 euros each, plus groceries. There was also a cleaning charge, as recommended by the owners, but that was out of the question. They weren't ready for third-party cleaning, or rather, Yamina wasn't ready.

Social evolution means her children are only just capable of entertaining the idea, which is already progress.

The next generation is bound to suffer less from poor person's complexes, and, as Malika says: 'One poor person is always reluctant to make another poor person work.'

Hannah has ordered her mother a Black&Green short-sleeved burkini, two-tone, for €23.89 from a Turkish Islamic clothing website: sefamerve.com. That way, she can swim in the pool while preserving her modesty before her children.

Yamina has never swum in her life. At seventy, she has never taken a dip in the sea or a swimming pool.

As a precautionary measure, Hannah has also bought a swimming belt and a foam noodle from Decathlon in Bondy.

The family convoy consists of two cars: Omar's Renault Talisman, and Hannah's blue Clio, diesel, 2006. Imane insists on travelling in the Clio with her sisters, sensing it will have more of a vibe than Omar's motor.

Hannah's USB key is plugged into the car radio, and throughout the journey the girls sing along to some good old French crooners, including Souchon, Cabrel, Nougaro and Brassens, as well as some bad old French crooners too, plus plenty of eighties' hits, and they belt out various raï numbers. Even Imane, who speaks broken Arabic with a funny accent, joins in. Malika loves teasing her about this: 'Each time you speak in Arabic, a sailor dies at sea.'

The girls stop twice at motorway services to quench their thirst and visit the toilets, which, contrary to popular opinion, are cleaner than at most Parisian restaurants.

In Omar's Talisman, they discuss politics, mainly, and listen to some surahs from the Quran. The Taleb menfolk talk about the strike, about pension reforms, about the Gilets Jaunes and which sections of French society are getting poorer year on year. They also talk about electric scooter accidents and Brahim forgetting his tube of Fixodent.

Omar tries to put his father's mind at ease, promising to replace the dental adhesive as soon as he goes shopping at the Intermarché a few kilometres from their rental home: *Together against expensive living, ta-dah!*

'I told you ten times not to forget your toothpaste,' Yamina tells Brahim, without looking at him, so distracted is she by the beauty of the countryside.

She can't take her eyes off the fields, never imagined that France had so many fields. There's no getting away from it, farming runs in Yamina's blood.

There's not a cloud in the sky, and a clear view all the way to the horizon. It makes a change from the washed out, urban, grey panoramas of Aubervilliers. Being on the road is a holiday in itself for Yamina, who is feeling giddy and elated.

She is filled with pride.

God knows, it's some achievement to raise your kids in a place where nothing was set up with you in mind, where you're a stranger to the codes. It is in the order of a miracle, and Yamina should be decorated with a medal, she should be crowned.

If she has held strong, it has been for them, so that they can succeed, so that they can do better than her and her husband, for them to be happy and, above all else, independent.

Yamina knows a thing or two about the price of independence.

She often experiences flashbacks to those first years at rue du Moutier; the scary men coming in and out of the old prostitute's place on the ground floor; Michelle, that was her name, a kind woman, who gave the girls presents every Christmas. Yamina thinks back to her ordeals with all those mice scuttling about the apartment, as if seeing cockroaches rising up from every corner wasn't enough.

Not one trap proved effective on the mice, they kept coming, and it drove Brahim crazy. Yamina can recall the time those wretched vermin gnawed their way through

Hannah's brand-new pair of trainers in the hall cupboard. And how her daughter burst into tears when she found her shoes destroyed on the day of an athletics competition. To think, she'd kept them specially to wear that morning for the first time. The word FLASH was written in red letters on the tongue of her cheap trainers, and Hannah liked to imagine that they would grant her the same superpower as the DC hero. She was bound to win the competition with her Flash trainers, netting the first prize, a voucher worth 200 francs to spend at Casino in Porte de la Villette.

Instead, she had to stay home with her mother because she didn't have another pair of trainers to run in. Hannah gave up on athletics for good that day.

No matter what Yamina did to make the apartment more pleasant to live in, it remained a hovel. Even when it was clean, it looked dirty, and it was so damp that their belongings had to be thrown away because of the mould. Yamina would take her children to the community health centre every week because they were always sick, an endless spate of sore throats and earaches, and in the dank apartment they could see the water trickling down the walls. Aged two, Imane asked her mother: 'Maman, why is the house crying?'

Yamina's worst memories are of the public baths on rue Henri Barbusse, where she would try to bribe the caretaker with a 2 franc coin, sometimes 5, in exchange for a few minutes more of water, enough to rinse off her daughters thoroughly, especially their long hair, which proved so time-consuming.

It made her sick at heart, but Yamina resolved to cut their hair, because of the panic around *the regulatory allotted time in the shower cubicle*.

The caretaker was an unsympathetic Portuguese woman with enormous glasses, who banged vigorously on the door with her fist. It made Iman jump every time. 'Open up, madame, finish, leave now, madame, go, go, go!' She kept repeating the same instructions, as if the Talebs were contestants in *The Crystal Maze*. Yamina barely had time to lather the soap on her own body.

In 1994, when they left their one-bed place on rue du Moutier for their current apartment at La Maladrerie, Omar was almost four, as Yamina remembers clearly. They had visited the four-room apartment, an HLM in this so-called 'sensitive zone' designated for urban regeneration, which looked like a fairy-tale castle to them. There was a bathroom, three bedrooms, and windows giving onto the street! Just like that, Omar stopped wetting the bed. 'House clean, Omar clean,' he told his mother.

Even as a little boy, he had a knack for turning a phrase.

Yamina sees a jumble of scenes playing out, a bulk batch of memories: the costumes she made for the end of year celebrations, the poems recited for Mother's Day, her tears of joy, leaving parents' evenings with her head held high, the enormous Saturday homemade pizzas Malika was mad about.

This is what is going through her head as she alternates between staring at her son's delicate hands on the steering wheel, and the thousands of sunflowers in the fields on her right.

Overwhelmed by the emotion of it all, she begins to cry.

For a long time, Yamina had been under the impression of losing out on so much, on time, on moments with her family, with her father, of being torn away from her land, her Algeria. How sorely she missed the fig tree of her childhood and yet, these days, isn't God offering her a new fig tree whose fruits are delicious?

Now Yamina has her children.

They are her recompense.

And they're taking her on holiday.

While Omar, Malika and even Brahim are doing the tour of the house, in a fever pitch of excitement, Imane and Hannah haggle over the bedroom with the en-suite bathroom.

As for Yamina, she takes out her compass from her black Quecha backpack, €3.90, to establish the direction of Mecca. She performs two rounds of prayers to thank Allah for his kindnesses, and to ask for his protection and mercy towards her family. *O Lord, when death comes for me, may it find my heart in the same state of peace as today.*

After a lunch of leek quiche and cucumber salad, and having first checked their father is taking his siesta, the girls run to put on their swimming costumes. Modesty dictates they can't show themselves in this apparel in front of Brahim.

To Imane's disbelief, Omar wears his tacky mauve trunks with the flowers. 'You're kidding me! You've still got those revolting things? The guy won't ditch his frumpy shorts!'

'Gotta make an effort, bro, now you've got a lady friend!' says Hannah, inadvertently delivering the scoop. Omar blushes. Hannah gloats. Malika's amused. Imane's figured it out. 'Aaaaah, so that's why you're glued to your phone these days!'

Malika finishes helping her mother put on her Turkish burkini. Yamina smiles awkwardly: the burkini is still quite clingy, and she feels embarrassed.

'Come on, don't worry, you look fab, and anyway nobody's going to see you, there's only your children here.'

And so, the mother of this family advances slowly, intimidated, towards the swimming pool steps, taking care not to slip, trying to mask her nerves, while Iman executes her first dive.

Hannah fastens the swimming belt around the waist of Yamina, who whispers: 'Don't let go of me, eh?'

Instinctively, the four children surround their mother in natural formation, as she ventures her first step in the water. Malika is leading her by the hand.

'*Ouh là là! Barda* – it's cold.'

Hannah is already all choked up at witnessing a moment which is, in her eyes, *historic*.

Yamina enters the water gingerly, clinging to the edge, then suddenly, and no one is expecting this, she bursts out laughing, a blend of fear and joy and excitement. Caught off guard, her children laugh spontaneously with her.

Hannah is laughing too, but there are tears streaming down her cheeks, and no one notices how emotional she is, her tears less visible on a wet face.

Yamina is six years old again, as if by magic, and it makes her kids gasp.

She glides slowly into the water, with Malika and Hannah supporting her on either side, helping her onto her back, in which position she is buoyed by the foam noodle.

As she looks up at the blue sky of the Charente, Yamina can't stop giggling. She is letting go, she feels free, and it's delicious, she has never tasted such happiness. She kicks her legs to give herself the illusion of swimming.

'*Ah là là, al-hamdullilah!*' she exclaims as she kicks.

Yamina can't get over being here, experiencing this moment.

Nobody for kilometres around, a large garden surrounding their house, fruit trees, nothing but fields as far as the eye can see. Not another human being, not since Catherine, the semi-deaf owner, showed up to give them the keys and run through the inventory in the late morning.

Seeing as she wasn't particularly friendly towards them, the Taleb children engaged in a quick debate. The perennial discussion: 'Racist? Not racist?' They put it to the vote: one for, three against. The theory of Catherine's deafness carried the day.

The vote against was, of course, Hannah's: 'Yeah, right, she can't hear, didn't you notice her giving Maman's hijab a dirty look, or the way her eyes could've burned holes in our cheque?'

'Racist? Not racist?' was a recurring question in the lives of the Taleb children. They were skilled players who could have devised a television game show format. 'Hello and welcome to Racist? Not Racist? Today, we're joined by an experienced contestant making his eleventh appearance and he's playing for the big stuff, yes, ladies and gentlemen, he's competing for a cash price of 25,000 euros! Bravo, Rachid! Let's give him a round of applause! Quick recap here: Rachid is a delivery driver who loves playing Loto Foot and eating honey cakes, he comes to us from Gennevilliers in the Hauts-de-Seine, and, in the first round he's up against Monsieur Blanc, a former overseas professional soldier, now based in Nice, whose retirement hobbies include collecting old-fashioned postcards and experimenting with electrical devices, which, he says, gives him a right buzz! Right, come on, Rachid, it's your turn to play! Jingle! Raciiiiiist? Not raciiiiiist?'

The Taleb children would rather not ask the question 'Racist? Not racist?' when there's something unclear in the way another person is relating to them. They would rather not waste so much time wondering where this patronising attitude comes from, or making the tedious connection with their heritage. Once in a while, they would also prefer to the luxury of denial, ignoring the scorn, as their mother does. The truth is, they would rather things were simpler.

Still, for a few days they're happy to discover a new face to the country where they were born, and even happier to be able to introduce it to their parents.

France is downright beautiful, there's no denying it, and when you travel through its towns and villages, its grand squares and small squares, it takes your breath away, and so how stirring it is, then, to understand its history and to tell yourself that you, too, are part of this, in one way or another, *whether they wish it or not*, and this history, well, you're the fruit of it, we're all the fruit of it, and one day we will finally admit this, and on that day things will become clearer for everybody.

Pillac is even better than the allotment at Aubervilliers.

Yamina has deserved this holiday, as well as this dip in the pool, offering, as it has, a sweet taste of childhood for someone who never really experienced childhood; above all, she has deserved all the love that is coming at her, she who has given so much and yet who has so much more to give.

You might say that Yamina has finished grieving, at last, for the impossible return.

Her home, and she understands this now, is where her kids are.

ACKNOWLEDGEMENTS

In memory of my father,
Abdelhamid Guène
(1934–2013)
who died of discretion.

To my mother,
to her heart which overflows like the Mediterranean.
With all my gratitude and love.
To her sacrifices which were not in vain.
The fruits of love grow on the generous fig tree.

To all those who inherit a history in fragments.

To the kids in anger.

To my heroine, Djamila Bouhired.

To the one and only, who I love and who has carried me
from the first line to the last.

To my daughter,
with all my love and my pride.

TRANSLATOR'S ACKNOWLEDGEMENTS

For Kate Elvins

And in memory of Emma Langley,
1983–2020,
friend, editor, game changer.
'What say?'